AN BARGAIN FOR A BRIDE

WESTWARD HEARTS

BLYTHE CARVER

A BARGAIN FOR A BRIDE

Cate Reed has one ambition. One dream. One goal. A theater in Carson City. How can they not have one? So uncivilized. This dream of hers goes against the grain of her sisters, and it seems of most polite society.

Polite society be damned, Cate Reed's going to get her theater, come hell or high water. Or a man who has a bargain.

Cate Reed's made a deal with a devil. A devilishly handsome stranger named Landon Jenkins.

Landon Jenkins needs an actress to perform the role of a lifetime. Is Cate that actress? And will she get what she wants or what she needs?

$$1$$

Cate walked the length of the room and back, her hands clasped behind her.

This was perhaps the most important speech she would ever make, one which could affect the lives of Carson City's citizens for generations to come. Nothing less than the future of herself and those many unseen people weighed heavy in the back of her mind as she stood, poised to deliver what she had worked so hard to prepare.

She cleared her throat, wishing her heart would not race so. Was she not an actress? Was she not a gifted orator? She had practiced delivering grand speeches before her sisters hundreds of times, perhaps thousands. This was nothing more than that.

With this in mind, she threw back her shoulders and imagined herself on stage. Prepared to hold an entire audience in her able grasp.

She came to a stop, lifted her chin and began. "Carson City is no longer a mere stopping point for travelers on their way to California, nor is it a town full of miners and those wishing to make their fortune in the mountains. Carson City is the capital of the state of Nevada and has grown exponentially in the last few decades. Its citizens come from all walks of life, both the highest echelons of society and those of decidedly lesser means. Travelers arrive every day on the train, both for business and pleasure. It is a bustling, thriving city, one which may not yet rival the size or sprawl of, say, New York City or Boston, but it very well could someday."

She thought that established her intentions quite admirably well. It was true that the town she had come to love was nowhere near as impressive as the larger cities on the East Coast, or even San Francisco to the west, but it was growing every day and had come such a long way since its humble beginnings.

It was enough to stir pride in her breast, the thought of how hard its citizens had fought to build the city into what it currently was.

"And just how does a city earn a reputation as illustrious as the cities I just named? The answer is twofold. First, it must establish itself as a center of business. This is what draws newcomers. The promise of prosperity. Farmers, ranchers, bankers and merchants, people from all walks of life have come here to make their home. There is opportunity here, especially with the advent of transcontinental rail travel. There is another hotel on the verge of opening in town, and new homes rising all the time. There is no reason for a man—or woman—of intelligence and industriousness to not make a fortune under such conditions."

She inhaled, then exhaled and lifted her brows.

Then she continued, "This leads me to the second quality a city must possess to rise above its humble origins, which is the presence of culture. Theater, music, art, and literature. It is these noble pursuits which men and women turn to once their day's work is through. It is through beauty and artistic stimulation that the human experience is elevated above those of mere animals. It is what separates us from them. We must have some grander vision after which to pattern our lives, and it is through the enjoyment of music and literature, and of painting and of sculpture that we derive that grand vision. It is through the vision of others and through their talent and dedication that life becomes more than simply the pursuit of a living. It is the reason we live at all."

Her heart always swelled when she reached that portion of her speech.

"Unfortunately, at this time, Carson City is sorely lacking when it comes to artistic vision. There is no cultural stimulation to be found. No opera house, no theater. No museums, no theatrical societies, no opportunity for arts and culture to thrive. Just as grass requires water and sunlight to grow, so do the human mind and heart require stimulation through the arts. By depriving Carson City's citizens of such stimulation, we deprived them of true satisfaction. Without a higher ideal after which to pattern one's life, it appears as though Mr. Henry Lawrence's saloon is the only refuge a man has from his work. Is it any wonder, then, that this establishment is so popular? When we give our citizens no other recourse through which to enjoy their leisure time?"

She shook her head, clicking her tongue mournfully. "This is why I propose the building of a theater in Carson City. This theater could not only mount dramatic productions, but it might serve as a music hall, a location in which town meetings could be held. In essence, a central hub around which Carson City's culture will spin. Perhaps the time will come one day when saloons and other such rough establishments no longer have a place here, for citizens will be too high-minded to ever stoop to such low diversions."

"I have attended theatrical productions in Baltimore, Philadelphia, New York, and Boston. The theaters in these cities are dazzling, drawing audiences like moths to a flame. It is in these hallowed halls that the audience is able to experience the fullness of life, the breadth, and depth of human emotion. They are able to lose themselves in a performance, to touch for a moment upon the fullness of the human condition, that which binds us together no matter our differences. They might even be able to understand life from the point of view of another, and they might carry that knowledge and understanding with them after the play has concluded."

She drew a deep breath, confident now.

"I believe we ought to see to it that our citizens are

granted the same opportunities as those in these cultural metropolises. I believe both they, and the city as a whole, will be all the better for it. That their children and grand-children will thank us for having the vision it took to make this dream a reality. The funding invested in this project will reap rewards far into the future. All we need now is the investment required to begin such a tremendous undertaking, and the bravery to see it through. Thank you so much for your valuable time and consideration in this matter."

She let out a long, shaky breath, a wide smile spreading across her face now that the deed was done.

"Well? What do you think?" She looked at baby Edward, seated in the center of her bedroom floor, who had so patiently listened as she practiced the speech she planned to deliver to her sisters.

He blinked, then inserted a thumb into his mouth.

"You're right," she decided before picking him up settling him on one hip. "Perhaps it should be a bit shorter, but I can't imagine removing any one part without losing the emotional impact. It is emotional impact which sways people. You must keep that in mind."

She walked him back and forth, going over and over the speech while doing her best to foresee any qualms her sisters might raise. They would have numerous objections, naturally. She was well accustomed to this by now, along with their disdain for her chosen profession.

It would not be easy to convince them to invest in the building of a theater once they came into ownership of the ranch and therefore were able to access the bank accounts their father had set up long ago. They would no longer need to rely upon the money their mother had left and might use it for this, instead.

From her perspective, this was an investment. As owners of a theater, they could only hope to reap dividends far into the future. After all, one of Mother's favorite lessons was the folly of placing all of one's eggs in a single basket.

Cate had always suspected, once she was old enough to understand, that her mother had been speaking from personal experience when she'd repeated this adage to her daughters. After all, she had thrown caution to the wind by cutting ties with her family and moving to Carson City upon meeting and marrying Richard Reed.

She'd staked her entire future upon their union. A union which had dissolved after less than ten years.

She has been fortunate that her family wealth was still present and accessible upon returning to the east, but there had been a few rather tense months in which even that had been uncertain. Only after admitting the folly of her marriage had she been granted access to her inheritance.

Cate imagined how this must have stung her pride, as Cordelia had always been a rather proud woman. But she had done it for her children, if not for herself, and afterward had made certain to teach her daughters to never rely on any one person or one set of circumstances to provide for the future.

She knew that if she put it to them this way, never mentioning her breathless desire to step out onstage and captivate audiences, they would see the good sense in her idea. They simply had to.

"After all, the townsfolk need a bit of culture," she reminded Edward before leaving the room and descending the stairs.

Rachel and Phoebe were in the kitchen, chattering excitedly. Cate assumed they were both in such high spirits thanks to their impending trip to town. They would spend the next three days with their husbands and were as giddy as schoolgirls in anticipation of their reunion.

"My goodness," she teased as she entered the kitchen. "One would think you've been apart for weeks rather than only a few days."

Phoebe rolled her eyes. "Wait until it is your turn," she warned. "A single hour will feel like an eternity."

Rachel nodded in agreement. "I would think that as an actress who is so understanding of the pains and joys and struggles of those around them, you wouldn't tease us like this."

"Perhaps it is all your fault," she suggested. "If any of you had taken me the least bit seriously in all these years, I might be a bit more understanding now. How do you like it?"

The pair of them merely exchanged a look.

Cate added, "You know I'm not serious. It disturbs me greatly for your sakes that you cannot be with your husbands all the time. Just think, it will only be another six months."

"It may as well be an eternity," Phoebe muttered.

Holly entered the kitchen, looking distracted, before finding Cate holding Edward. "There you are," she said, coming to them with her arms extended. "I've looked all over the house for the child. I should've known you were practicing your theater speech in front of him."

Cate blushed painfully. "Were you listening at the door?"

"I didn't have to. I merely needed to be on the second floor, where your voice rang out. You do not need to shout, you know." Holly pulled a curl from Edward's fist. He seemed to enjoy pulling hair and did not care whose dark brown locks he happened to be holding.

She blushed harder than ever. "I was shouting?"

"We could hear you from down here," Rachel smirked.

"My favorite part was the one where you talked about the human condition, and how a theatrical performance can unite an audience in spite of their differences," Phoebe giggled.

This was too much. "Once again, none of you take me seriously."

"It isn't that we don't take you seriously," Holly assured her with a pat on her shoulder. "It's simply that your vision is a bit grander than your means. The building of a theater is a tremendous undertaking, which will require an entire team of architects, builders—"

"To say nothing of the work it takes to put on a performance," Phoebe added. "There are people who build the sets, people who arrange for costuming and hairdressing and facepaint."

"And the selling of tickets, and the printing of hand-bills," Rachel supplemented.

"You wish to create an entire business," Holly concluded. "You are not simply erecting a building."

"This is something we can all do together," Cate insisted. "Once we have ownership of the ranch, it isn't as if our lives will change so very much. Lewis will continue to oversee operations. Roan will train the horses. The ranch hands will go about their work. We will still have nothing to do."

"Nothing to do?"

Cate turned, her heart sinking at the appearance of her oldest sister in the doorway.

Molly folded her arms, her mouth set in a firm line. "Perhaps you ought to try your hand at another profession, if you find yourself with nothing better to do but make up speeches. Rousing speeches, I will grant you, but a waste of your valuable time, nonetheless. Even when we come into ownership of the ranch, it isn't as if we will be surrounded by luxury. As you say, nothing will change. Including use of the money in the bank. That money is to be used for the ranch, and to support us. Nothing more."

"And what if I sell my part of the ranch? What if I allow the four of you to buy out my portion of the inheritance?"

"Are you sure you want to do that?"

Cate should have known Lewis would be just behind her sister, as he tended to follow her wherever she went now that she was carrying his child. If he could have wrapped her in paper and set her away as if she were some fragile piece of china or crystal, he would have done just that.

"And why not?" she challenged, hands on her hips.

It always turned out this way. All of them were against her, just as they had always been. They all felt they knew best just because she was the youngest, and because she possessed imagination and a flair for the arts, unlike the rest of them.

"Has anyone ever told you the fable about the goose who laid the golden eggs?" Lewis asked, going to the coffee pot to pour himself a cup. "If you were to sell your share of the ranch to your sisters, certainly you would wind up with a great deal of money, but it would be less than the amount of money you would collect from the ranch's operations over the rest of your life."

"There would be no further money coming to you, either," Molly warned.

"I would invest in the theater and collect the profits from that," Cate argued.

"If the theater is profitable," Molly argued in return. "I'm sorry, but I cannot allow this. And I'm tired of hearing talk of it, to be honest. Life in the theater is no life for an honest, virtuous young woman like yourself. It's downright scandalous that you even consider it. I'd hoped you would grow out of the idea by now, but I see I was wrong."

They were all against her. Just as they had always been. They were either deliberately blind or simply determined to circumvent her at every turn. Regardless of the reason why, it left her heartbroken.

They were all happy. Even Phoebe and Rachel, although they could not see their husbands every day, thanks to the terms of their father's will, stating they must maintain residency at the ranch for one year before inheriting it.

Otherwise, they all had what they wanted.

None of them understood Cate wanted what she knew would make her feel as fulfilled as they did. It would never be enough for her to simply marry and keep house. The first time Mother took her to the theater, she'd known without a shred of doubt that it was the life for her.

All her sisters could do was stand in her way and criticize, determined to make her believe her dreams were unworthy of pursuit. She would've thrown herself into a chair and wept if she thought for a minute they wouldn't call her a baby.

There had to be another way, and she was determined to find it.

She'd show them if it was the last thing she ever did.

2

———

"I shall drive the buggy into town and bring it back this evening."

Phoebe and Rachel exchanged their second troubled look of the day.

"This is a sudden announcement," Phoebe murmured, arching one eyebrow.

"I agree." Rachel tilted her head to the side. "What brought this on? You stormed from the kitchen less than an hour ago, swearing one day you would show us all."

Cate put on her most contrite expression while biting the side of her tongue to keep it in place. Yes, she'd spoken in haste and feared she would come to regret it before long. Only once she'd cried her eyes out in the privacy of her bedroom had she begun to think clearly again.

And she'd begun to plan.

Her plan led her to the bank, but she needed a reason to go to town. What better reason was there?

"I thought I owed it to you after teasing about Rance and Mason," she murmured, still contrite. "Besides, I could use a bit of time outside in the fresh air. And a chance to say hello to my brothers-in-law."

"You're up to something." Phoebe's eyes narrowed. "I feel it."

"I am not!" Cate insisted, reminding herself not to protest too much and give herself away. "I wish you had a bit more faith in me. What could I possibly be up to?"

"I'm afraid I don't care very much, either way. I want to be with my husband by supper." Rachel motioned to her valise, packed and ready to go.

Phoebe would not be so easily put off, however. "You look awfully nice for a quick ride in and out of town," she observed, eyeing Cate's grey woolen tea gown and fur-trimmed hat and cape. All of them were new, purchased especially for the coming season from the dressmaker in town.

"Since when is it a crime to dress nicely when one is about to be seen in town?" She turned in a circle, arms held out. "You never know when I might catch the eye of some eligible young man. Just because neither of you cares for such things any longer does not mean I have put my heart to bed."

Phoebe giggled at this. "I see. Your kindness is nothing more than a ploy to lure a potential suitor."

Cate merely shrugged, smiling slightly. Let her sister believe this was all in service of finding a husband. It was safer for her to believe that than to know the truth.

Roan was on his way out to the stables when he happened to find the girls preparing to leave and was kind enough to load their things into the rear of the buggy. "Do you have enough blankets? Hot bricks for your feet?" He'd lived so much of his life in the wilderness, facing harsh conditions, and tended to be a bit overprotective when it came to ensuring the girls' safety and comfort.

"Yes, yes, Molly saw to it." Cate patted his arm with a smile. "You might tell her when you see her, or Lewis, that I have taken the buggy out to drive the girls into town."

"Perhaps you can stay for supper?" Rachel asked, climbing into the buggy.

Roan's brow knitted. "Do you think it would be wise to bring the buggy back at a late hour?" Ever since Holly was kidnapped by men along the road into town, the men of the ranch were more concerned than ever for the safety of the women. It was after escaping her kidnappers that Holly met Roan, her husband of only two weeks.

"You make a good point. You're welcome to stay, Cate." Phoebe joined Rachel, the two of them waiting impatiently to be on their way

Yes, perhaps it would be for the best to spend the night in town. She might have more time at the bank and not feel quite so rushed. Besides, there was no guarantee that anyone would be able to see her immediately. If she had no choice but to remain in town until it grew dark, she would have to explain to her sisters why she'd been so late and why she needed to spend the night. This way, she already had that problem taken care of.

It seemed things were lining up in her favor. She took this as a good sign and climbed into the buggy with greater confidence than ever.

"Yes," she decided as if she'd deliberated at all. "Please tell Molly and Holly that I will spend the night in town and return tomorrow."

They tucked the blankets around themselves, hot bricks warming their feet, before Cate tapped the reins against the backs of the chestnut mares hitched before them.

Indeed, this was how she would make her dream come true. She would go to the bank and implore them to provide the investment for the building of a theater. That was what they did. Was it not? This would be an investment for the entire town, and any business person worth their salt would surely see it.

That was the problem with going to her sisters. They could not see beyond the ends of their noses and were unable to rid themselves of the notion that acting was, on the whole, a profession far beneath her.

She managed to join in the happy chatter as the team whisked them away from the ranch. Even in spite of her excitement and nervous energy, she felt a sense of gladness for her sisters. They were so clearly overjoyed at the prospect of being with their husbands again.

She wondered—vaguely, in the back of her mind— whether she would ever experience such deep, abiding love.

No, she did not want that yet. She wanted to be an actress, and an actress could not tie herself down to housekeeping and childrearing. She needed to be free, to travel and perform and touch the lives of countless audience members. Just the thought of doing so sent a thrill through her.

"Allow me to take the reins," Phoebe offered. "You must tuck your hands beneath the blanket for a time."

Cate gladly relinquished the reins and did as her sister suggested. While it had already been cold upon leaving the ranch, moving as swiftly as they did only made the chill feel more pronounced. She tucked her chin beneath her muffler and huddled close to Phoebe, with Rachel doing the same on the other side.

"We'll need the sleigh soon," Rachel called out from behind her net veil. "I hope we do not have a harsh winter. I would hate to think of trying to make this drive through deep snow."

"We shall think warm thoughts, then," Cate decided, and the three of them laughed.

It had always been this way. Even the most contentious mornings invariably gave way to warm, friendly afternoons. No matter how they fought, and no matter how often her sisters teased her and disapproved of her choices, Cate knew that at the heart of everything was a deep well of love.

They passed the rest of the ride this way, the three of them taking turns with the reins, until the familiar sight of the town's buildings became clear on the horizon. The flag flying above the state capitol building waved in the wind, an ever-present landmark which guided travelers coming from all directions.

Anticipation thrummed through Cate's veins, sending her pulse racing wildly. She fought to keep her excitement under control, unwilling to give herself away. They would surely wonder why she was so thrilled over the prospect of spending an evening with them and their husbands, and she could only tell so many lies convincingly.

Though she suspected neither of them would care much, either way, seeing as how they were too involved with their own romantic concerns.

The men were at the jailhouse, as they normally were during the day, so Rachel and Phoebe planned to get to work preparing supper soon after arriving at the little house belonging to Rance. "I hope Mason and I are able to have a little house like this one day for ourselves, wherever we go," Rachel confessed as they descended from the second floor where she'd left her bag to be unpacked later.

"You don't think you'll stay on the ranch?" Cate asked.

"Even if we stay in the Carson City area, I can't imagine Mason wanting to live in the big house," Rachel shrugged. "Besides, I think every woman wants a home of her own, to run as she sees fit. Phoebe and I have already butted heads enough over the management of this house, and we are only here for half the week."

As the house truly belonged to Phoebe, she felt as though her decisions ought to be final. Rachel, on the other hand, had ideas of her own. But Mason's future had not yet been decided. Would he wish to return to his uncle's detective agency in Pittsburgh once Rachel's year on the ranch was up? It had seemed unwise for them to purchase their own home just yet.

Cate could not understand what was so difficult about managing a household, and what could possibly inspire the two of them to fight as they had over it. Chores were chores. Cooking was cooking. What else was there?

It was already past two o'clock, and Cate knew she had to get to the bank quickly or else risk being put off until the following day if the men working in their offices were too busy to speak with her. "I believe I shall take a walk down Carson Street. That is, if you don't mind. I can return soon to help with supper if you wish."

Once again, Phoebe eyed her with suspicion. "Are you meeting with someone? Is that why you were so eager to come with us today?"

"Yes, why are you so set on getting away from us now?" Rachel asked as she tied an apron around the waist of her striped work dress.

Both women had changed out of their heavier woolen clothing now that they were inside the house and working in the warm kitchen.

She found herself at a loss for an explanation. Luckily, she did not need to provide one.

There was a knock at the kitchen door just a moment before it swung open, and in bounded Jesse. "Aunt Phoebe!" he shouted before throwing himself at her, flinging his arms about her waist and squeezing hard. "I lost a new tooth!"

"Another one?" Phoebe asked, examining his mouth. "If you don't slow down, you'll have no teeth left at all!"

Martha chuckled upon entering the kitchen. Her son always managed to run ten steps ahead of her, no matter where they were going, and as such, his arrival nearly always preceded hers. "We saw you ride past and there was no keeping him away," she offered by way of apology. "You know I would rather give you the chance to settle in before coming for a visit."

"Nonsense," Rachel chided with a smile, pulling an extra teacup from the shelves, along with a tin of cookies.

"Just think, we shall have to begin the Christmas cooking and baking soon," Phoebe murmured with a gleam in her eye and a quick glance Jesse's way.

The boy's eyes widened as he imagined all of the good things which would come out of their kitchen. "I can help!" he offered. If he'd licked his lips, it would not have come as a surprise.

Cate joined them in laughing merrily, then slowly backed out of the kitchen as the women engaged in conversation. Only four days had passed since they'd last seen each other, yet it might as well have been a lifetime.

She was glad they'd found a good friend in town and was even more glad for Martha who'd been rather lonely after the death of her husband.

But at the moment, she was most glad for the diversion. Were it not for Martha's timely arrival, she might need to explain the importance of getting to town. She fastened the large, shiny buttons of her coat, wrapped her muffler around her neck and tucked the ends into her collar before affixing a fur hat in place and sliding her hands into her seal skin muffler.

It was always good to make a fine impression when going on such important errand.

And this was perhaps the most important errand she had ever gone on in her life. Nothing less than her entire future hung upon this visit to the bank.

Her footsteps were quick as she walked from the house down the three blocks between it and Carson Street. So long as neither Rance nor Mason stopped her going into the bank, she would be safe.

And once she got there, it seemed an inevitability that a sensible man would see the potential in her idea.

The bank sat catty-corner from the jailhouse, and she cast a watchful eye in that direction before turning toward the large, stone building with gold-painted letters spelling BANK above the front door.

She realized with a start that she'd never been inside a bank before. There had never been a reason to. Molly had always taken care of the banking in Baltimore, and now Lewis managed things for them. She had no doubt she and her sisters could manage for themselves were not for the way men tended to look down upon women as being less capable. Lewis had warned early on that the bankers of Carson City were more likely to take seriously a man's presence than that of a woman.

She only hoped that was not the case today.

It was dark inside. The glass shaded lamps at each

worker's window giving off little light beyond that which the men behind the counter needed to see by. She counted no fewer than five brass spittoons as she crossed the marble floor, and that plus presence of thick, almost choking cigar smoke spoke of a heavily male presence in the place.

She did her best not to wave the smoke away nor to cough visibly, smiling at the first man who caught her eye. Now that she was here, her knees quaked terribly. Good thing her heavy skirts and coat concealed this as she marched over to where the young man in question stood behind the brass grate which ran the length of the counter.

"I would like to speak to someone in regard to an investment," she announced, reminding herself that an actress could portray any emotional or physical state of being. She needed to be confident now, so she did her best to pretend to be.

The young man—he might have been no older than she was—wore a pince-nez on the bridge of his nose through which he peered at her as if he didn't believe she existed. His hair was slicked down with pomade, gleaming even in the dim light from the lamp positioned beside him. "An investment, you say?"

She nodded, eager now. He hadn't told her to leave, which she took as a good sign. "Yes. I wish to open a theater here in Carson City and would like to speak to someone in relation to securing the financial investment needed for such an undertaking." She was quite proud of herself for sounding as though she knew what she was talking about.

The man blinked, clearly surprised by her forthrightness. "I... That is, it..."

She waited. When the gentleman did not continue, she prompted, "Is there someone here I might speak to?"

"What's this all about?" An older man appeared, emerging from an office behind the row of clerks. The cigar wedged firmly between his teeth belched blue-gray smoke her way, which she struggled not to choke on as she raised her chin in what she hoped was a confident gesture.

The young man paled slightly, turning to the older man and murmuring something close to his ear.

The older man paused, then, withdrawing the cigar from his mouth, laughed heartily. "You say this young woman is here to ask for a loan?"

Rather than waiting for the young man to answer, Cate spoke up. "Yes, that is exactly why I'm here. My name is Cate Reed, of Reed Ranch. My father was Richard Reed."

"Yes, yes, we are all well aware of who you are, Miss Reed. And of your parentage. However..." The man's face went red as he laughed again. "We are not in the business of extending loans to young women. Do you have a husband to speak for you?"

A husband? Indignation filled her head, threatening to spill out of her mouth. A husband! "I have not," she muttered, her teeth clenched though she bared them in a smile. "I have a mouth of my own and can speak for myself."

"Well, I'm sorry, but you'll need a man to take out a

loan," he snorted, shaking his head and laughing again as if he'd heard the funniest thing imaginable.

By now, he had alerted half the bank to her presence and to his dismissal of her. She felt their eyes on her, the eyes of so many men, and she wished she could sink into the floor and never return.

For they were not kind eyes, not kind men.

They considered her nothing more than a silly girl. Some of them even chuckled, shaking their heads at what they perceived to be her foolishness.

She could do one of two things in this situation. She might either stay and stand her ground, demanding he grant her the chance to speak her mind as a future landowner and account holder with the bank.

Or, she could turn and run, wishing she'd never made such a foolish mistake.

Pride demanded the latter, and so she turned and stormed out with all the dignity she could muster while her dreams fell to pieces all around her.

It was never to be. She would never see her dreams become reality. Why did her sisters get what they wanted most while she could only grasp at smoke?

A phosphate at the druggist's might soothe her sorrows. She could not possibly return to Rance's home in this state. Her sisters would know in an instant that she was upset and would pester her until they found out why.

One day, when she was on stage, she would recall this dreadful embarrassment and use it in a performance. Otherwise, this would all have been for nothing, and she would have no one to blame but herself for the laughter which echoed in her head.

"Excuse me, Miss?"

She was so upset, her hands shaking inside her muff and her knees trembling almost too hard to support her, that she almost did not hear the man who approached from behind her.

"Miss? Cate Reed, was it?"

She whirled around, prepared to give this man a piece of her mind. Now that she had been turned down before she could even present her speech, there was no longer any reason to keep the social niceties in mind. "What? Did you follow me out here so you might laugh at me, too?"

He took a backward step, frowning. She took him in with a practiced eye. He was rather handsome. Dark hair just visible from beneath the brim of his bowler hat. Full lips on a firm mouth. Blue eyes which she now discovered seemed filled with concern.

He was well-dressed, right down to the gold pocket watch on a gold chain visible thanks to the fact that he had not buttoned his overcoat before following her outside.

"I had not intended to laugh at you," he assured her. "My name is Landon Jenkins, and I believe we can help each other."

3

———

"Thank you for agreeing to sit down with me." Landon studied the girl now that they were seated in the back corner of Ruby's Restaurant, as private a setting as he could imagine on the spur of the moment.

His first impression of her at the bank was of a naïve, headstrong young thing who'd worn her finest clothing as a weapon against the snide, patronizing men in the bank. That was what they were. They dismissed her without waiting to hear what she had to offer.

Now he saw that she was, indeed, young. Also very pretty, with her shining brown hair and sparkling dark eyes. Outrage, embarrassment, and chill in the air had lent a pink tinge to her cheeks.

"I would like some tea," she murmured, eyes sweeping the room before darting out the window and surveying the sidewalk beyond. It was mid-afternoon and thus not very busy, with most people hard at work.

"Are you looking for someone?" he asked after a minute of her staring outside.

Her eyes met his, then lowered to the tablecloth. "My brothers-in-law work here in town, and I ask myself if they might see me here. They will naturally wonder why I've sat down with a stranger."

"Who are your brothers-in-law?"

"Sheriff Connolly and his deputy, Mason Murphy."

Landon's eyes widened. Of all the people, she had named two of the most respected and most powerful men in town. They might not have been captains of industry, but they could easily throw him in a jail cell if they decided he'd taken liberties with their sister-in-law.

"Goodness," he said with a chuckle. "I had not expected that."

She tilted her head to the side, her eyes narrowing in skepticism. "You heard me use my name in the bank. You do not know of the Reeds? Or Reed Ranch? I had assumed that nearly everyone in town knew of us and our situation."

"Perhaps I would if I had been in town over the last year, but alas. Business has taken me to Chicago and St. Louis, then out to New York. I have only returned this past week."

"Oh, I see." She tapped her fingers against the table, still anxious. "Why did you ask me to come here with you? What is it you think we can do for each other?"

"I do appreciate frankness." He smiled, hoping to encourage her to relax and warm up to him. He'd need her to be relaxed and open to suggestion if he was to make this work.

He questioned whether his impulse had been the right one, whether he made a mistake asking her to join him. While his heart had gone out to her in the bank—truly, they had behaved abominably toward her—he'd seen opportunity the instant she'd stormed out.

She needed money. Money was something he had in abundance.

Now, seated across from her, he asked himself whether he'd lost his mind. Simply a temporary lapse in judgment, brought about by lack of sleep and constant strain in the week since his return from a long journey.

It was the strangest and most ill-advised idea he'd ever come across, which was saying something based upon the ideas he'd had in the past. He was known as a man willing to take chances, and that combined with sharp instincts had built his fortune.

Were his instincts correct about her, however? Pouring his money into a business in which he saw potential was not the same as wagering on a person. People were far less predictable than businesses.

He supposed there was nothing to lose by presenting her with a wild notion which had crossed his mind the instant before he ran from the bank to catch up to her.

He asked the waiter to bring them a pot of tea and a pot

of coffee before clearing his throat and folding his hands atop the table. This was a business proposition, nothing more. He had presented propositions to men worth millions of dollars. He could certainly speak to this young woman.

"You say you need money. Why, exactly? How do you plan to use it?"

Her chest puffed out. "I intend to open a theater in Carson City. There is a woeful lack of culture here, to the point where I am surprised others consider this a civilized place at all. Surely, sir, in your travels, you have come to know the difference between Chicago and St. Louis and Carson City."

This was surprising. A theater. He expected her to speak of a dressmaker's shop or some such feminine enterprise. But a theater? "Are you a member of the theatrical profession?" he asked, doubtful.

"I intend to be."

So that was it. He bit back a smile for her sake. This was a young woman of great pride, pride which had already been wounded deeply. "You intend to be the main attraction, then," he surmised.

"Were it not for the fact that I was called upon to come to Carson City and spend a year here, I would already be a member of a theatrical troupe which had passed through Baltimore on its way north to Philadelphia. I had intended to leave with them, not knowing at the time that my father would pass away out here, and I would be called upon to claim my inheritance. The terms of his will state that my sisters and I need to live here for a solid year, or else all five of us forfeit ownership of the ranch."

He remembered Richard Reed. Things were beginning to make sense. Only a man as coarse and miserly as Richard Reed would think to keep his daughters in Carson City for a year before they inherited what was rightfully theirs.

"I see. To be honest, I agree with you. There is a lack of culture here. I would enjoy the opportunity to attend a play or an evening of music. I'm sure the women's group here in town would appreciate a venue for their dramatic readings and whatever little things they put together." He hoped he did not sound dismissive.

Her eyes lit up, and she leaned forward slightly. He got the sense that it was rare for her to find someone who agreed with her.

"Precisely. Which is why I believe such a building is needed here. It will benefit everyone, not merely myself or other actors, but the entire city. That terrible man at the bank would not even listen to reason."

"Worse than that. In order to listen to reason, he would have needed to take you seriously. Which he certainly did not do."

She sank back in her chair, more miserable than ever. "I know," she murmured. "I'm accustomed to this. Goodness knows my family has never taken my dreams seriously. This was my last hope."

He did feel sorry for her. Though her problems were not his problems, and his problems had been keeping him awake throughout the night for an entire week.

She wanted a theater. He had the money. He was more than gladly give to her if she would help relieve the strain.

The coffee and tea arrived, and he allowed her time to add milk and sugar to hers before speaking again. "As I said outside, I believe we can help each other."

She lifted the teacup to her lips, arching one eyebrow. "Oh? I did not get off the train this morning, Mr. Jenkins. I'm well aware of what strange men who offer young women great amounts of money have in mind."

It was a good thing he had not yet taken a sip of his coffee, for he would have spat it out across the table before laughing at her insinuation. She was a clever one; he had to give her that much. And courageous considering her willingness to march into a bank where she knew no one, where it was all but an inevitability that she would be turned down.

She had done it nonetheless and maintain her composure throughout.

"I'm afraid you have misunderstood me. I have nothing unsavory in mind."

"How do you intend to help me, then? And what would I have to do in exchange?"

"You see, I have found myself in quite a predicament." And it only occurred to him then that she might be scandalized by what he was about to say. She gave him every impression of being a well-bred woman, and she had spoken of living in Baltimore and was the heiress to a ranch. This was no low, common girl who might be more understanding of his regrettable folly.

She waited, brows lifted.

He swallowed and suddenly wished his collar was not so tight. Perhaps it was embarrassment making him so uncomfortable. He had every reason to be embarrassed, for he had behaved abominably. "As I said earlier, I have been away from Carson City for nearly a year while attending to business. Before I left, I was in the process of courting a young woman who lived just outside of town. We enjoyed each other's company very much, though I made it clear to her that I would be away for a year and did not expect her to maintain any unfortunate emotional ties to me." Oh, this was even more uncomfortable than he had ever imagined.

Mainly because the girl refused to take her eyes from him once he had begun his story. If only she would not look at him the way she did, studying him and forming unspoken opinions behind those clear, startling eyes of hers.

When she did not say anything, he continued. "Upon my return last week, she paid me a visit." Perhaps he should have ordered something a bit more soothing than coffee, for his hands trembled tellingly. "With her was a baby. Two months of age."

He stared at her, waiting for her to understand.

It was clear when she did, as her eyes went perfectly

round and she drew a deep breath. "*Your* baby?" she whispered.

He merely nodded.

"Yes, mine. She knew not where to reach me when she discovered she was..." He grimaced, unwilling to speak the word, but the girl understood. "Naturally, I would have done the right thing by her if I had known. In fact, upon her arrival and her announcement, I was willing to make things right. I had never intended to settle down into marriage, but I am not a man who runs from his obligations."

"I suppose you expect me to find that admirable," she murmured.

"It is immaterial to me whether you find it admirable or not, but I did feel you ought to know my intentions. As I was saying, I was prepared to do the right thing by her, but she refused."

Cate's eyes opened even wider than before. "Refused? What is she thinking?"

"Your guess is as good as mine, as she left town. I invited her to spend the night in a spare room in my home, as she arrived rather late and it was quite cold, and neither she nor the child were dressed appropriately considering the weather. I thought we could settle things in the morning, make plans. When I awoke, she was gone. But the baby remained. I learned from the stationmaster that a woman matching her description took the train that very morning."

"Goodness gracious," Cate whispered, shaking her head

with a hand pressed to her heart. "She must have been quite desperate to do anything of the sort."

He should have known she would take the girl's side, as any woman would. Truthfully, he would have felt the same sympathy for Ida were he not utterly exhausted and at his wit's end after receiving his father's telegram that very morning.

"Now, I have a child to care for. One without a mother."

She clicked her tongue. "I feel sorry for the little one. What is her name?"

"Violet," he said. He detested the name and had already considered changing it. But that was far from the worst of his concerns. "I have business to tend to, an office I must visit every day. I have a housekeeper and cook, but she is far too old to address an infant's needs. Several women have come in and out over the last week to care for her while I work, but it is not a good long-term solution. However, that is not what I asked you here."

"I had assumed you wanted a more permanent caretaker for your child," she admitted.

"No, I'm sure I could manage somehow. The real problem arose this morning with a telegram from my father. He's a... Senator from Massachusetts, where I was born and raised. I doubt you would be aware of him, but he is quite a powerful and well-respected man. And he announced to me this morning that he and my mother plan to visit in a week, after a series of conferences and meetings in California are finished."

"Oh."

He waited for her to say more, but she remained silent.

"I assume you understand the awkwardness of my position. I certainly cannot present my child without a mother to go along with her, nor can I admit the circumstances of her birth. It might even cause a scandal for my father, which I'm afraid to say he would find unforgivable. I'm trusting you with this information, and I hope you keep it between the two of us."

"Of course. I understand how devastating this could be for all of you. I have yet to understand what it has to do with me, however."

He leaned forward, elbows on the table, whispering. This was where his entire ill-formed idea would either solidify or fall to pieces. "I need a wife. Only for a short time, only as long as my parents will be in town. I need to present the image of happy home for their sake—along with concern for my father's reputation. Not to mention, my mother has been quite ill over the last few years. If anything, knowing her son finally settled down and started a nice family would be a comfort for her."

Once again, understanding dawned on her lovely face, but this time, outrage soon followed. "You expect me—"

He held up a hand, knowing she was about to blurt the whole thing out rather loudly, for anyone to hear. "Please, let us be discreet."

She pursed her lips, furious, then whispered, "You expect me to pretend to be your wife? You intend to give me the money for the theater for that? You can't be serious!"

He was afraid her eyes might fall from her head.

"That sounds to me suspiciously similar to the reaction those men had in the bank," he pointed out. "You judge my idea unthinkable before you have given it time and consideration. Please entertain the notion before declaring it impossible."

That gave her pause. She blushed, lowering her eyes, twisting a delicately embroidered handkerchief between her equally delicate hands. "I still find it hard to believe you would support my plans in exchange for something which should only last..."

"No more than a few days," he assured her. "My father is a busy man, and he is continuing on to Washington after our visit. He and my mother are unable to be present here during the Christmas holidays, so this is their way of at least spending a bit of time with me my father's schedule demands he move on. There is absolutely no chance of them extending their visit, so you need not worry about this taking longer than it needs to."

Then, he added what he knew well might be the final nail in the coffin. The point at which she would run away.

"We would need to be married by the Justice of the Peace. I cannot merely pretend to be married, in case someone were to find out this is a lie and report back to my father or—even worse—his political rivals. It might kill my mother, knowing I'd brought a woman in to live with me without the benefit of marriage. The entire thing can be annulled later, naturally. I will hold you to nothing and will gladly provide all the backing you require for your theater."

She blinked, her mouth hanging open. Not a word came out.

In fact, he asked himself whether she was breathing. Had he shocked her that badly?

Perhaps her nerve only extended so far. Perhaps going to the bank that day had been the end of it.

"Well?" he asked. "Will you become my wife for the sake of your dreams?"

4

Cate knew not where to begin.

She sputtered, completely at a loss. It was rare that her quick mind could not arrive at an understanding of any problem, no matter how enormous that problem happened to be.

This? This was nothing she'd ever encountered.

He looked at her, expectant. Wanting her to give an answer right away. How was she to give an answer to such an outlandish request? Was she to have no time to think it over? Not even time to consider the many, many ways in which this could go terribly wrong?

"Let me make certain I understand you," she managed to say after a moment of sheer panic. "You expect me to live and act as your wife—"

"Oh, goodness no. No! I expect nothing of the sort." To his credit, he managed to appear embarrassed. "You need

only stay with me at my house while my parents are visiting. There will be no other, eh, you know. Duties."

That was a relief, at any rate.

Her cheeks flushed, her skin crawling with shame,
nonetheless. Marital duties. At least she would not be
required to perform them.

"All right, then. But I will be required to sign my name
to a marriage license, I would imagine. We will legally be
husband and wife."

"Yes, yes, but as I said—"

She held up a hand, and he went silent. "Do not speak
over me right now. I am trying to make sense of this. If you
truly require my assistance, you will allow me to make
sense of it without interrupting. Do you understand?"

It occurred to her only once she'd finished that she
might have offended him.

Instead of becoming indignant or, worse, causing a
scene by walking out and leaving her there alone, he
nodded. He was a businessman, after all, and could clearly
understand when it was time to allow his potential partner
to make a decision.

Only what decision would she make?

On one hand, it seemed the easiest thing in the world.
Simply a matter of being married for a few days, taking
care of a darling baby. She had always loved babies, after
all, and could only imagine this one was a darling little
thing. A few days of work and she would have the money
she needed to make her dreams come true.

He did not expect anything of her, outside of her willingness to pretend. Well, to pretend and legally marry him, but he did promise an annulment when all was said and done.

Truly, when she looked at it this way, it seemed too easy for words. In fact, she considered herself foolish to even take the time to think it over. Why think it over? She would never get the money otherwise.

On the other hand...

Molly would kill her. Pure and simple, she would kill her. Such a sudden marriage would bring scandal down upon the family, setting tongues wagging throughout the town. Phoebe was married to the sheriff, Rachel to the deputy, and all of them would be the subject of scrutiny thanks to gossiping old biddies who made their point to know everyone's business.

How could she possibly hope to keep this a secret? That would be the only way to avoid utter ruination, if she could keep this quiet. It would mean a great deal of planning in advance, but they had no time.

If she were to go through with it, she would need to jump in feet first and hope to manage as best she could as they went along.

Was she actually considering this? Such a wild proposition. Marrying a perfect stranger for the sake of appearances. Saving his father's reputation and his mother's health.

Think of the money, think of the money. Think of the theater. Think of your dreams.

When she considered the countless hours she spent

imagining herself on stage, in front of an adoring audience... Those dreams would die, would wither and shrivel and fall to the ground to be trodden underfoot without the money required to create her theater.

And since Holly and the others had reminded her that she would be creating a business, the idea had lodged itself in her mind, unwilling to let go. She would be a businesswoman, not merely an actress. She would oversee everything, would reap the rewards once she made a success of things.

She knew she could do it. She only needed the opportunity.

The opportunity was before her, in the form of a handsome, wealthy young man in trouble.

Though much less so in trouble than his unfortunate friend or his child had suffered. The poor girl had fled under the weight of shame and scrutiny.

Men would never understand what it meant for a young woman to be in such a condition. Cate's sympathetic heart went out to the girl, imagining the strain she'd been under as she tried to locate the man to whom she had surrendered her virtue.

Cate had never been in the presence of someone who'd fathered a child out of wedlock. Rather, she was never aware of having been in the presence of such a man. He did not seem a bad sort, and she did believe he would have done the right thing if allowed to do so. If the girl had not left, none of this would be a problem for him.

Then again if the girl had not left, Cate would not be on the verge of getting everything she ever wished for.

There was something else to consider, as well. The baby. Poor little thing, passed around from one caregiver to another. That was no way for a child to grow up, even though the little thing was too young to understand. The thought of caring for her, even for a short while, warmed Cate's heart and made the prospect of marrying this man seem much more agreeable. Fake marrying, she reminded herself.

In the back of her mind, she knew she would become attached to the wee little thing just as Holly had become attached to Edward before marrying Roan. It was simply something she would have to endure.

"Well?" Landon prompted. "Do you have any further questions? Is there something I can clarify for you? Or shall we move ahead?"

She laughed, a bit breathless. "You do march forward, sir. I feel a bit breathless, as if on a train which suddenly began speeding headlong, without a way to stop it. I would hate to make the wrong choice."

"The only wrong choice in this situation would be if you were to say no. Please, hear me out," he added, noting her scowl. "I dislike putting it to you this way, but there is no way you would ever obtain the money to open a theater without my assistance. While he might have exercised better judgment in delivering disappointment, the man at the bank was correct. The law states you need a husband to sign papers for you if you are to obtain the loan. Even if you were married to some young man, he would need to have the means or the property required to put up as collateral against such a large sum."

"I have a ranch. Or, I will have it soon enough."

"But the ranch is not completely yours. The bank cannot possess merely a fraction of the ranch. How many sisters do you have?"

"Four," she reported, her heart sinking.

"The bank will not accept one-fifth of a ranch as collateral. You would need to put up the entire property."

"That will never happen."

"I had suspected as much, and I don't blame you. Even if you were set on doing so, I would advise against it. That is a great gamble."

She sniffed, unimpressed. "I suppose you are rather proud of yourself, putting me in a corner this way. You know I have no choice but to accept, though I do not in any way understand how we will make this work. I know nothing about you, and you know nearly nothing about me. We will need to make it look as though we've been married at least long enough to have created child together."

He nodded, pensive. "I understand. I have a few days in which to work it out. I have no doubt that I will be able to think of something. I know my father, and my mother. I know what they'll want to know, I know what they will ask. I believe I can predict their questions and come up with answers. Of course, all of this is predicated upon the ability to sleep, which I have not been able to do for a week."

She grimaced. "The baby keeps you up at night?"

"Does she ever. Even with the help of some understanding friends of my housekeeper, there is still little to be done about a crying baby who refuses to sleep through the night. I have done what I can to assist, to make things easier, but she seems determined to keep us all awake."

"Babies will do that I suppose," she replied, feeling no small amount of sympathy. He might have behaved indiscreetly and gotten a young woman in trouble, but she'd left before he found a way to make things right. The fact that he had not turned the baby over to an orphanage or found some other way to rid himself of it spoke to his character.

He fixed her with an intense gaze, his square jaw hardening as he grew serious. "I need to know. Every minute we sit here is another minute in which we might be learning more about each other and finding ways to make our marriage appear legitimate. I will write up a quick contract, if you desire. We can both sign it. In it, I will detail what is expected of you and what I will give you once the deed is done. There is little more I can say, other than to urge you to make up your mind. We might even be able to get to the justice of the peace before he closes his office for the day."

She blinked rapidly, unable to keep up with the pace of his thoughts. "Today? This afternoon?"

"Of course. Why not?"

"I—I don't know. This is all happening so quickly."

He nodded, yet appeared unmoved. "You cannot tell me anything I don't already know. Yes, this is happening quickly, but everything has happened quickly in the past week. I arrived home from a long trip, utterly exhausted from travel and looking forward to nothing so much as soaking in my own tub and sleeping in my own bed. Instead, I was introduced to my daughter that very evening. My entire life has changed. I know all too well what it means to have that happen. But your life need not change so much, not for such a very long time. I will be a father for the rest of the child's life, which will extend past my own, God willing. You merely need be my wife for a week."

A week. Just a week.

She could keep this from Molly and the other girls for a week, couldn't she? She was clever. She had imagination.

And when they asked her where the money came from, she might tell them...

After the annulment had been decreed, of course. There would be nothing left to lose by then.

"Might I ask one favor?" she asked before finishing her tea.

"What is it?"

She was already in the act of putting on her gloves. "I would like to see your house. And your baby."

5

L andon could not pretend to understand why this was so important to her, but he opened the front door to his home and ushered her inside.

He was not certain what to expect from her in terms of a reaction, considering the fact that she lived on a sprawling ranch. He suspected his home, while large and quite comfortable, was nothing in comparison to hers.

"It's quite lovely," she said, looking around. "It could use a woman's touch, but I suppose that's to be expected. I also suspect your mother would instantly note the lack of it."

His palms began to sweat. "What do you mean?"

She lifted her shoulders, her head moving back and forth as she looked in one room after another. The parlor, his study. A library. The dining room, even the kitchen. The entire first floor was empty at the moment, which made him suspect Mrs. Davis was upstairs with Violet.

Perhaps she was sleeping, which would be a blessing.

He had already heard her crying throughout the night and was not sure he could stand it during the day, as well.

Cate returned to the parlor and stepped inside this time. "For instance," she began, running her fingers over the top of a small table, "there is a noticeable layer of dust here. I suspect your housekeeper has been overwhelmed and unable to perform her duties as she ought to. Or perhaps, she never was, to begin with, and you simply did not notice because you are always so busy with your work. There are no embroideries anywhere, not figurines or flowers or any sort of ornamentation that a woman would want in her home. If we were to have been married long enough for me to be the mother of your child, and for the child to have been... conceived while in wedlock," she managed to choke out, turning her back to presumably hide the embarrassment on her face, "I would have established a presence in this home. It feels very male, very masculine."

"See? I never would've known it. I am so glad to have chosen you, as you can help me make this more believable."

She turned to him now, in the act of rolling her eyes as she did. "Please, do not insult my intelligence by pretending you chose me carefully. I was simply in the right place at the right time, and you happened to overhear my distressing situation. Nothing more than that."

He nodded. "Fair enough."

She returned to her assessment of his home. "I suppose I might be able to add a few things here and there, and while I am here to take care of the baby, your housekeeper will be able to perform her work more thoroughly. We ought to be able to bring this place up to snuff by week's end."

"We? Do you mean to say you accept my proposal?"

"I would like to see the baby." She removed her gloves, then her hat, placing both on a table by the front door before beginning her climb upstairs. "I assume she is up here."

She moved so quickly, it was a struggle to keep up.

He bounded upstairs behind her. "Mine is the front bedroom, with a door which connects it to the next room. That is the room in which the child has been sleeping."

Cate nodded before opening the door, as confident as one would be while moving about their own home. The fact that she had already made herself so comfortable gave him hope.

Just as he had suspected, both the baby and Mrs. Davis were asleep in the big bed, with the old woman snoring as she dreamed. This was intended to be the separate bedroom of a wife, though he had none to speak of.

But he did believe in being prepared, and a such had seen to its furnishing upon moving in.

Cate shook her head as she crossed to the big, four-poster bed. "I have no experience with such small babies," she whispered, "but it seems to me the child needs a crib, or something similar. Do you mean to tell me she sleeps in the bed with her caregiver? It is a wonder she hasn't been smothered!"

She did not wait for him to offer a reply before picking Violet up from the bed. He had to stop himself from lunging forward to stop her. After all, she was finally asleep, and he did so miss being able to hear himself think while in his home.

But Violet did not stir. She slept peacefully, content and warm.

Cate looked down at her, running a gentle hand over soft, blonde curls. "My goodness," she whispered.

There was a softness in her voice now that he had not heard before. She had taken to the baby just as he'd known she would. It almost seemed unfair, as if he used his child against her when he did not.

At least, it had not been his intention.

Now? He knew she wanted to accept.

She cast a doleful look to the bed, on which Mrs. Davis continued to snore unaware of their presence, then motioned for him to join her in the hall. She continued to hold Violet, either refusing to let her go for fear of being in danger of the sleeping woman, or simply because she longed to hold her.

"I can see this child is in dire need of help," she whispered. "It's nothing less than scandalous, the fact that no one thought to provide this child's needs. Goodness gracious."

He couldn't help but bristle at her imperious tone. "I thought you said you were not an expert."

"I'm not. Which makes my ability to see how little thought has been put into her care even more surprising.

I'd think an old woman such as your sleeping house-keeper would know this little girl needs a great many things. They do not have to be fine things or fancy things, but she needs a crib. She needs clothing and smaller blankets and my goodness, what have you been feeding her?"

At least he knew the answer to this question. "She gets milk in a glass bottle with a rubber... device." He could not bring himself to use the word "nipple" in front of her.

She nodded, frowning. "Yes, I suppose in the absence of a wet nurse that would be the only alternative. And if you were to bring in a wet nurse, that would be one more person who knows a child born out of wedlock lives here. You don't want that. All right, so long as everything is perfectly clean while in use, she should be all right."

"How do you know so much about this?"

She rolled her eyes, shaking her head as if she suddenly found herself speaking to the most ignorant person alive. "I might be the youngest of my family, but I recall many after-noons in which my mother sat with her friends around the card table. They spoke of all manner of things, and while I was not supposed to be listening, I could never help myself."

"Because you wanted to learn how to care for a child when your time came?" He found something charming in the notion of a young girl wanting to prepare herself for her vocation.

She snickered, shattering his illusions. "No. Because I wanted to know everything there was to know about motherhood, in case I was ever called upon to play the role of a mother."

He stared at her, unable to determine whether she was telling a joke or not.

She scowled. "It's true."

He managed to keep from laughing out of sheer desperation. She was quite an odd one, but he had little choice. Time was running out. "Well, no matter the reason, I'm glad you know what you know. As you can see, I spent the last week trying to keep things afloat. I've been so overwhelmed that I have not had a chance to plan."

She looked down at the baby again, stroking the fine, soft curls on the top of her head. Her hair was still quite short and sparse, naturally, but he'd already stroked it and knew from experience just how soft it was.

"I do know what it feels like to be overwhelmed," she admitted, never taking her eyes from the child.

"If we are to do this, we need to do it today. We must move forward. As you can see, there is a tremendous amount of work that needs to be done before my parents arrive if we are to put on a good show of it."

She chewed her lip, her brow wrinkling as she thought it over one last time. He was ready to burst with frustration. If only she would not keep him hanging on tenterhooks.

Either she would do it or she would not, and she'd already given him the distinct impression that she intended to go through with their arrangement. He merely needed her consent.

With a sigh, she nodded. "All right. So long as we can

keep this secret from my family. I'm entirely uncertain of how I will, but I'm sure I can think of something once I put my mind to it. I see no reason why we cannot be successful."

He had never known such relief. "Thank you, thank you so much."

"Yes, well, I will be getting something out of the arrangement, too." She nodded toward the bedroom. "I suggest you wake your housekeeper and tell her we'll be going out for a bit. I truly would rather she not sleep next to the baby that way. I once heard a story of a woman who accidentally smothered her child while sharing a bed, and it has never left my memory. I would so hate to see something like that happened to this little one, especially when you have the means to provide something safer."

"I'll see to it."

Anything she said, anything at all. She'd agreed to help him, and that was all that mattered.

Twenty minutes later, they stood in front of the Justice of the Peace. This woman who was a stranger to him, who he only knew as Cate Reed—originally of Baltimore, Maryland and now of Carson City, Nevada—was about to become his wife.

He did not even have a ring for her, though he supposed that was for the best for now. He might be able to purchase something before his parents arrived, but it would not do for her to be seen around town wearing a wedding band.

The thought of the sheriff and his deputy arriving at his

front door with their weapons in hand was never far from the forefront of Landon's thoughts.

For her part, Cate looked calm, serene. He suspected she imagined herself on stage, performing some grand role, prepared to bring her audience to tears.

She held his hand as the vows were read aloud, with not one but two perfect strangers who worked in the office to witness their nuptials.

"I do," she whispered. There was no mistaking the catch in her throat. Here she was, marrying a man she had not known the existence of until two hours earlier. He suspected she must want her theater very badly if she was willing to take such a large step.

"You may kiss your bride," the judge said, smiling at Landon as if the two men shared a happy secret. As if Landon even knew this woman.

But the judge was not aware of this, and so there was no choice but to turn to his new bride with what he hoped was a loving smile.

He found her eyes filling with tears, and for the briefest moment, he truly felt for her. She'd more than likely imagined her wedding many times over, especially with married sisters of her own. He suspected this was nothing like the weddings she had witnessed, nothing like the dreams she'd had.

Had she ever been kissed? He might be the first to kiss her, and under such dubious circumstances.

With that in mind, he was gentle and respectful as could be, barely pecking her lips.

She deserved much more than this, and he felt like a cad. Even more so than he had when Ida arrived with Violet in tow.

"Thank you, Mrs. Jenkins," he whispered with a smile.

She tried to smile back, but it was shaky and weak.

There was no going back now.

6

What had she done?

She was married. And a stepmother, technically.

Meanwhile, Phoebe and Rachel were waiting for her back at the house and expected her to eat supper with them.

What had she done? What was she going to tell them?

She pulled up short just as they were about to leave the judge's office, the enormity of what she had just embarked upon hitting her all at once. "Well, my goodness," she whispered, her eyes darting around as she searched for somewhere to sit.

She needed to sit.

She needed to breathe.

She needed something to drink.

"Do you think you could fetch me a glass of water?" she

whispered as she sank onto a leather chair positioned by the door.

Landon looked at her in alarm. "Of course," he said.

The judge's secretary poured from a pitcher before handing her the glass.

Her hands shook so.

Landon crouched before her, helping her hold the glass steady while she raised it to her lips.

It felt as though she was moving in a dream.

She barely felt the water as it poured into her mouth and down her throat.

She barely heard him murmuring words of encouragement, asking her to breathe slowly and take her time.

Take her time?

The very concept struck her as highly amusing, seeing as how she'd only just leapt into marriage with a man whose middle name she did not even know.

After taking several deep breaths, she nodded. "I'll be all right," she said, and the strength in her voice surprised her. Perhaps she would be all right, after all.

Until Molly got wind of it, however. And then there was no telling what she would go through.

No, Molly could never know. None of them could.

But how could she hope to accomplish this without her sisters being aware? She needed an accomplice, but who?

"Are you able to stand?" Landon asked, concern in his voice.

He did have a gentle way about him which she appreciated. She needed a bit of gentleness after what she'd just done and before what she would need to do now.

"Yes, thank you." In spite of her assurances, however, he helped her to her feet and took her arm in a solicitous gesture as they left the judge's office and walked down a wide staircase leading to the exit which looked out over Carson Street.

She supposed a husband would do that for his new bride. Helping her walk, keeping her steady. Though she could not imagine a typical bride suddenly collapsing out of panic mere moments after her wedding.

"There are things I didn't tell you, things I did not think of until now," she murmured as they walked. The moment they were outside, she shook her arm free of his grip. "We cannot be seen together like that in public," she warned him.

"Of course," he murmured, taking a step away from her so as not to inspire curiosity. They were mere acquaintances, nothing more. "What are you only just now thinking of?"

"My sisters. I must find a way to get around them. If none of them are going to know, I must have an excuse. You see, according to the terms of my father's will, we must maintain residence at the ranch. I told you this."

"Yes, and you also told me two of your sisters married men from town."

"They split their time between their home in town and the ranch," she explained. "Perhaps if I'd had enough time to put this together in my head, I would've thought to tell you this. I'm going to have to return with them at some point. I cannot spend the entire week here. If anyone from the bank were to find out and know that I have not been living on the ranch, they might use this as an excuse to say that one of us has been in breach of the will's terms. They will look for any opportunity to take the ranch from us. I cannot allow that to happen to my sisters."

Though Holly was able to get away with it for two weeks, was she not? Though knowing Cate's luck, her situation wouldn't turn out so happily.

"I do wish you had mentioned that before."

"If you would give me time..." She shook her head. "There has to be a way around this. As it is, tonight I need to go to my sister's house. I'm expected there. I can't avoid it if I wish to avoid uncomfortable questions."

What a wedding night this was. She would not even be afforded the chance to enjoy a wedding supper with her husband.

But he was not really her husband, was he? They were strangers and they would remain strangers until their annulment, at which point they would go their separate ways, but not before she got her money.

"You might prepare that contract tonight," she reminded him. "I can come tomorrow to sign it."

"You truly intend to go back home tomorrow? How are we supposed to get to know each other?"

He had a point. Was there any way she could think to arrange for more time in town?

It was clear. She would have to tell someone about her problem. She would need a partner.

Would it be Phoebe or Rachel?

Regardless of who she chose, the result would be the same. She nodded, looking up at him as they walked back toward the center of town. She clenched her hands tightly inside her muff, digging her nails into her palms to keep herself calm. What an unholy mess she'd gotten herself into, but it was all for a good cause.

If only she could keep reminding herself of that.

"All right. I will speak to one of my sisters tonight and ask for her assistance. She might well be able to help me come up with story that will suffice. Perhaps I can pretend I have an ill friend here in town who needs help. A friend with a baby who is too ill to care for her."

"Would you have such a friend without your sisters knowing about her?"

She let out an exasperated sigh. "Would you let me worry about that? Do you not think I already know how tenuous this idea is without you reminding me? I must do what I must do. Simply leave it to me. After all, what's the worst that could happen? I'm married now. I have a husband who will stand up for me."

She couldn't help but laugh at the expression of pure horror on his face. Even while looking horrified, he was still rather handsome. She supposed she could have done worse for a fake husband.

"I'm only teasing. You'll have to get used to that if you are to be my husband."

He groaned. "I mean no offense, but this week can't end quickly enough."

"I quite agree." They came to the corner on which the bank sat, and she nodded, as if on the verge of saying goodbye to an acquaintance. "Mr. Jenkins, I will see you soon. As early as tomorrow morning, but not earlier. I'm afraid I cannot spend the night at your house without my brothers-in-law suspecting something. As far as they are aware, I will go home tomorrow. Only my sister Phoebe need know that I have remained in town."

Because it would have to be Phoebe. For she possessed the romantic heart it took to understand the situation. She would feel desperately sorry for both the mother and the child and might even be stirred to sympathy for Landon.

Perhaps if she was busy feeling sorry for everyone involved, she might be too busy to deliver the sound thrashing Cate suspected she deserved.

"That sounds fair enough. In the meantime, I will see to it that a crib is delivered to the house as soon as possible. Perhaps I can find something suitable at the mercantile for now."

She shook her head. "Purchase a basket with handles," she suggested. "Something that can be placed on the floor or carried through the house. It will look suspicious for a man who is, according to most of the town, unmarried and childless to purchase a crib. I might look for one tomorrow, as it is less suspicious for even an unmarried woman to make such a purchase. My oldest sister is expecting. I can use that as an excuse."

His eyes widened, and he looked a bit perplexed. "You seem to think of everything."

"Yes, I have trained my mind to be agile and to find quick answers to problems. After all, one never knows when disaster will strike on stage, and an actor will have to contrive a coverup in front of the audience and make it appear as though nothing is wrong."

To his credit, he didn't laugh at her as her sisters would have. He merely smiled, touching his fingers to the brim of his bowler. "Good day to you, Miss Reed."

To her astonishment, he winked, and a smile played at the corners of his mouth.

As if this entire thing was amusing. As if there were anything to laugh about.

As if she did not now need to explain this to Phoebe in a compelling enough manner that her sister would not strangle her.

And to think, she had only just been practicing her speech in front of Edward at the house. Little did she know that by the day's end, she would need to make a much more important speech.

There was much more at stake here than funding for a theater, no matter how important that funding was.

Important enough to lure her into marriage with a perfect stranger

Though it was not entirely for the sake of funding that she'd married him. Violet needed help. She needed the guidance of a woman with a head on her shoulders, as the women who Landon had tasked with caring for the infant were clearly not up to snuff.

She wondered whether this Mrs. Davis had ever borne a child and suspect that she had not, or she would have seen to the purchase of a crib for the child long before this.

Poor thing. She would need stability in her life, and there was no hope of receiving it in such tenuous circumstances. Cate could only hope that with time the situation would settle down, Landon would grow into the role of fatherhood and would be able to secure better care for his daughter.

Her stepdaughter. What an entirely strange concept that was.

Now, she would be able to act as a mother should the situation call for it because she'd been a mother. If only for a short time.

"Where were you?" Rachel demanded, coming from the kitchen at the sound of the front door closing. "We were about to send word to the jailhouse for Rance and Mason to look for you."

Oh, goodness. To think of what might've happened had she done that. "All is well, no need to worry about me." She knew she sounded too excited, her voice too loud and an octave higher than usual.

She took her time of unbuttoning her coat, breathing deeply and slowly as she did. She simply had to calm herself if she was going to avoid uncomfortable questions.

The girls had already all but settled the question of supper, leaving Cate to set the table.

When Phoebe entered the room with a pair of candles in silver candlesticks, she cast a meaningful look her way.

"I need to talk to you," she whispered with a glance toward the kitchen. "Alone."

Phoebe chuckled. "I knew it. I knew you were up to something."

"It's nothing like you think. It is nothing I could have predicted upon leaving the house earlier, I swear it. I'm afraid I got myself into a bit of a pickle, and I'll need your assistance if I'm going to make it out without the rest of the family knowing."

Phoebe's face fell. "It's that serious?"

"You have no idea."

She looked up at the ceiling, most likely offering up a silent prayer. "Rachel, can you keep an eye on the stove? I will go upstairs and unpack my valise, and I might do the same for you, if you wish."

Rachel called out her agreement from the kitchen, and the two of them went upstairs where they might have a bit of privacy before the men returned from work. The bedroom Phoebe and Rance shared was charming, and it was clear upon entering that it bore the marks of a feminine presence. Cate had been right about that. She knew she'd been.

She ran her hand over a lace-covered pillow while Phoebe closed the door. "What have you done?" she whispered, turning on the oil lamp which sat on the heavy, old-fashioned dresser.

"Let me start by saying that I did not see any other way

out of the situation. It seemed this was the best chance I had of getting what I want while helping someone in need."

"What have you done?" Phoebe repeated, staring at her with her arms folded.

Cate knew it would do no good to tell her how much she looked like Molly right now, so she held her tongue. No sense digging her grave any deeper.

There was nothing to do but get it over with. "I got married."

Phoebe went silent for so long, Cate feared she had shocked her into a state of catatonia. "It isn't permanent; we'll get it annulled. You see, I met a man today in town—"

"You. Got. Married?"

Cate nodded. "At the Justice of the Peace. Let me explain, please. We will have it annulled, I swear. Only this young man—"

Phoebe held up both hands, her head shaking back and forth so rapidly her features nearly blurred. "No. No, no, no. You are not telling me this right now. I must be imagining things."

"For heaven sake, I need to explain. Please, just stop talking long enough for me to get the story out." She took Phoebe by the arms and sat her on the bed before explaining herself. She told her about the trip to the bank, admitting that she had in mind all along, then explained how Landon had found her and offered her the money she needed in exchange for marrying him.

"It is only for the sake of his parents, nothing else. Well, as far as he's concerned. The baby truly needs a woman in her life, if only for a short while. The poor thing is suffering while he scrambles about madly, trying to understand what it is he needs to do. He has no one in his life tell him how to conduct himself, and his mother certainly cannot do it because she needs to believe the child was conceived and born in wedlock. Do you understand?"

Phoebe's mouth hung open, her eyes wide and, Cate suspected, unseeing. As if she had gone far away in her mind rather than staying and listening and understanding the enormity of Cate's dilemma.

"I need your help."

That seemed to shake Phoebe from her shock. "My help? How could I help you with this? When you have gone and done the most terrible, cotton-headed thing you ever done your entire life? I could never imagine something like this, nor could any of the others I wager. My goodness, you want me to be party to this?"

"You already are, because you know about it."

Phoebe threw her hands into the air with a sharp laugh. "Thank you. Thank you for making me part of this when I have no desire to be."

"It isn't that bad. You're making it out to sound as though I killed someone."

"You might kill someone. Molly might die of shock, after she kills you."

"Let us not be overly dramatic."

"That is easy for you to say, as if you're not the most dramatic person I've ever known. To marry a complete stranger!"

"I only did it to help him."

Phoebe snickered. "And to help yourself. Don't pretend this had nothing to do with your desire to open this theater of yours. If it weren't for your fool notion of becoming an actress in the first place, none of this would've happened."

"Yes, but then again, I couldn't get what I want. I want this theater. You know how important it is to me. If I can get what I want while also helping someone else, I see nothing so terrible in it."

"Does the sanctity of marriage mean nothing to you?"

"This is merely a business arrangement. We will not actually live as man and wife. For heaven's sake, Holly lived with Roan for two weeks before they even came to the ranch. I didn't see you causing such a fuss about that."

"Holly did that because she had no choice. It was either live with him or freeze to death. This is hardly the same situation, so do not pretend as though it is."

"What of Landon's mother? Her health is poor, and he's afraid she will worsen if she learns her grandchild has no mother."

"That isn't your problem! And it's still not the same as Holly saving her own life, so stop." Phoebe looked away, her chin trembling. "I cannot believe you. I cannot believe you would do something like this."

"Phoebe, please." Cate sank to her knees, taking Phoebe's hands in her own. "I need you to understand me. I need you to help me. This need not affect any of us."

Phoebe sighed, sounding and looking more unhappy than Cate could ever recall. It was her fault, a fact which was not lost on her. "You're asking me to lie to my husband, do you realize that? He certainly cannot learn about this. No one can. This will lie so heavily on my conscience."

"I'm sorry. I truly am. Were this not all so rushed, I might have had more time to think it through."

Phoebe smirked. "Don't bother with your pretty lies. We both know you would've done it anyway, because it will help you get what you want. I must say, I knew this theater meant a great deal to you, but I had no idea you would go to such lengths to obtain the money for it."

"I wish there was a way for you to understand. When I held little Violet, I felt so sorry for her. Truly, Phoebe, if you only knew. No one there knows how to care for a child. No one even suggested the child have a crib or any sort of sleeping arrangement. She is being passed around to whoever might have a spare evening to help care for her, and nothing more. Landon certainly hasn't the first idea what to do with her. If I can at least take a week and teach him that he needs to know—I'll grant you I am no expert, but it seems I know more than all of them put together—I might be helping Violet get a better start in life. The man has plenty of money, but absolutely no common sense."

"Common sense, eh? Do you think you are the person to be speaking poorly of someone's common sense?"

Cate held her tongue, for this was not the time to start an argument. "All right, I will give you that. But surely you must understand what I mean. Please. Help me, if only for her sake. Once all is said and done, I vow I'll make it up to you."

Phoebe snickered before turning back to Cate with a sigh. "I will have to do a lot of thinking to come up with something to match what you're putting me through."

"And I promise to accept whatever it is you come up with." Cate threw her arms around Phoebe, her heart lighter than it had been since before the wedding ceremony.

Until the downstairs door opened and the sound of men's voices floated up through the floorboards.

This marked the beginning of the greatest performance of her life.

7

"And you can sign here whenever you've finished. If everything is to your liking, that is."

Landon handed the pen to Cate, who ignored it in favor of reading his contract. It was simple, detailing what would be expected from both of them. He took the opportunity to sink into his favorite wing chair, close to the fire in his study. At least Mrs. Davis had seen to that upon her arrival this morning. The poor woman's normally neat, prim bun of steel-gray hair looked a bit looser and sloppier every time he saw her.

His life was not the only one turned around thanks to the baby's sudden presence.

"There is no actual sum named here," she pointed out, frowning when she looked up from the desk, and the contract spread out over the top. "Is that a mistake?"

"I couldn't say out of nowhere how much it would cost you to erect a theater," he admitted. "And I wouldn't want to hold you to a certain figure, then find out you'll need much more. That hardly seems fair."

Her brow creased as she appeared to study him. "Hmm."

"Hmm? What does that mean?"

"It means I'm a bit surprised at your fair-mindedness. You seem to take me into consideration, which I hadn't expected."

"Why wouldn't you?"

"Landon." The way she said his name. As if speaking to a willful child. "I don't know you."

"Oh. That is true."

"I have little reason to expect you to keep me in mind, and I appreciate that you are. So you've said here that you intend to provide anything and everything within reason, upon conferring with architects and builders."

"Correct."

"And that if any unforeseen changes were to occur, you would manage those as well."

"Also correct." He yawned, near the point of exhaustion after yet another late night.

"Forgive me if I'm boring you."

"You know I'm tired because of the baby," he grumbled. "Can we get on with it? Forgive me, but we have a great deal more to discuss."

"Of course, of course." She sighed, shaking her head and muttering to herself, but at least she went back to reviewing the contract. He warned himself against taking issue with every little thing she said and did, or else he might have asked what she was muttering about him.

Was this what it meant to have a wife? Learning to hold his tongue even when she muttered and whispered to herself about him?

"I see nothing wrong with this," she declared upon finishing. "But before I sign, I want you to know that I've brought my sister Phoebe into this scheme."

"How did she react?"

Her expression—dismay, chagrin, sheepishness—told him everything. "Between the two of us, we decided it hardly seems right for the baby to continue here while I return to the ranch to keep up appearances."

"We still haven't decided what—" He sat up, fatigue forgotten for the moment. "Wait, you want to take the baby with you?"

She nodded, surprisingly eager. "Yes, I believe it's a good idea. You see, I can tell my sisters that my friend is ill and cannot care for her baby while she recovers. Then, after a few days, I can come back. In time for your parents to arrive. It will grant you a little time to rest, too. See? It works for everyone."

He wished he felt as positive as she sounded.

Yes, the notion of a few nights of sweet, unbroken slumber appealed greatly. He never thought he would come to miss sleeping so much.

But...

He'd already come to love his child. He understood this now, while facing the prospect of being without her for only a handful of days. He hardly knew Cate, and he certainly knew nothing of her family.

"How do I know she'll be safe there?" he countered.

Cate's brows lifted. "Because I say she will," she replied, cool and perhaps a bit insulted.

"I don't know if that's good enough."

"And I don't know if your promise to grant me an annulment is good enough," she spat.

"It's in the contract."

"Fine."

To his surprise and perhaps horror, she picked up the pen and scribbled something at the bottom of his contract.

As she wrote, she murmured, "I hereby promise nothing will befall the child, Violet Jenkins, while she is in my care at Reed Ranch."

With that, she signed her name with a flourish. "See? Now it's in the contract. Which I have signed to prove how serious I am."

What could he do? "Very well, then."

"You'll let me take the baby with me when I go home?"

"I don't see myself as having much of a choice."

"It's for the best."

"You seem to believe that."

"I do, because it is. This gives me a reason to return, and it gives you the chance to get your house in order while I'm gone without having a baby to consider."

"Get my house in order? What does that mean?"

To his surprise—truly, he knew he ought not to be

surprised when his new wife was involved—Cate withdrew a folded slip of paper from the pocket of her woolen coat.

"What's this?" he asked when she handed it to him. He would certainly need more sleep if he was to keep up with her.

"A list of items you need to purchase for the home. I went through it with my sister, who has already set up housekeeping in her own home and understands these things better than I do. She, too, had the task of taking her husband's home and making it her own. He'd lived alone before marrying her, and thus lived as a bachelor lives. The way you have."

"I see." He went down the list, frowning as he did. "What on earth do I need china figurines for?"

"Oh, good grief. I can take the list to town and see to purchasing what you need, if that makes it easier for you."

"No, you would need to put everything on my account, which means providing an explanation. I believe I can manage this, perhaps with the assistance of the new shop-keeper's assistant. She seems very eager to please her customers."

A silence filled the room.

He looked up from the list to find her scowling. "What? What did I say?"

"You can't speak that way in front of me," she warned. "A husband would never say such a thing in front of his wife unless he expected a sound thrashing. Besides, you had better start behaving like a married man, even if you don't reveal our marriage to anyone. Do you understand what I mean?"

"Who do you think I am? I hardly make use of the upstairs rooms at the saloon," he snarled.

"But you intended to flirt with the girl at the mercantile, did you not? So she would assist you in locating what I listed?"

He couldn't deny it, so he chose to remain silent.

She looked downright smug. "I thought so."

"You needn't scold."

"I am your wife."

"You married me. You are not my wife."

She slammed her palms down on the desk, sending him reeling back in surprise. He'd never expected that sort of display of temper from an otherwise mild-mannered, well-bred young woman.

Just who had he married? Perhaps the old adage was true. Marry in haste, repent at leisure.

She shot up from the chair, eyes blazing. "We are supposed to act as if we are husband and wife, yes? I am trying in every way I know how to remind you of that fact, yet you seem determined to undermine me. Do you want to convince your parents or do you not?"

He wished she didn't look so beautiful when she was furious. The extra color in her cheeks and the flashing fire in her eyes struck him as being almost painfully alluring.

"You are the actress," he murmured by way of acquiescence. "Proceed."

This mollified her somewhat, and her nostrils no longer

flared like those of a bull when she sat again. She ran a hand over her hair, smoothing it back in its coiled braid which shone in the light from the window behind her.

A woman of contradictions, to be sure. On the surface, she was everything she ought to be, well-groomed, lovely. Wearing tasteful, stylish clothing. Some women could wear the most lavish garments yet appear cheap and vulgar, nonetheless. Not this wife of his.

It struck him then that were she not such a flighty thing, full of strange ideas and even stranger habits. Imagine, listening in on private conversations so she might more accurately portray a character one day. She might make some man an excellent wife. She possessed a sharp mind, was efficient and energetic.

So long as the man in question had the patience of a saint, their marriage would be a great success.

Once she'd regained control over herself, she continued, "As I said, see to the purchase of those items, please. Take special consideration of the items for the baby, which is its own section of the list."

He'd just gotten to that. "She needs all of this?"

"I thought you had the means."

"I do," he grumbled, waving her off without looking up from the paper. "I'm simply surprised by the amount of preparation necessary. You're certain she needs this?"

Cate rested her chin on her palm, gazing at him. "You are a well-to-do businessman. If this were the daughter of a farmer, it would make sense for her to wear a simple, homemade nightgown of old scraps from the rag bag. What she wears now is the garment an unmarried, friendless young woman would sew for her baby. You cannot allow this to continue."

He saw the sense in this and wished it were not up to a complete stranger to set him straight. She humbled him with her ability to see through the fog which had enveloped him the moment Ida announced he was a father. "Very well. I shall see to all of this just as soon as possible."

"Good." She stood up like a shot and was halfway out of the room before he could react.

"Where are you going?"

"To see the baby, naturally. I'm simply aching to."

"Wait, wait." He scrambled out of his chair and followed at a fast clip. "She only just got to sleep."

"That is very nice. I'll be careful not to wake her." She eyed him as they climbed the stairs side-by-side. "Shouldn't you be on your way to your office by now?"

Drat. He glanced up at the grandfather clock at the second-floor landing. It was already well past eight o'clock. "I can wait a few minutes more," he decided. "They'll hardly close down the company without my being there."

She giggled softly. "I thought all important men of business were certain their employer would fall into ruin without their presence."

Mrs. Davis was awake this time, and she looked downright sheepish when Cate entered the bedroom. "I'm sorry, Miss, for not having been able to meet you yesterday," she whispered. "This wee thing keeps me on my feet much of the time."

"I understand," Cate smiled before nodding in approval of the large, deep straw basket he'd purchased the previous afternoon.

Violet slept in it, nestled into a pile of blankets, her tiny fists hands resting on either side of her head.

His heart lurched violently. He was supposed to allow her to leave his house? Such a small thing, so easily harmed. Utterly defenseless.

Cate leaned over her, her thumb stroking the tiny fingers which opened reflexively, then closed around her thumb and squeezed. She gasped, a wide smile lighting up her face. Pure joy. "She's very strong, isn't she?"

Her eyes met his, shining and warm, and he suspected he might be able to trust her. That she might have fallen in love with his daughter, just as he had.

It was a start.

8

―――――

"I wish you wouldn't insist on my coming with you," Phoebe hissed as they walked side-by-side from her home to Landon's. He lived on the fashionable side of town, the side where no sheriff could afford to live.

It struck Cate as being terribly unfair that a man who oversaw the safety of an entire city could not afford to live in a house like Landon's. Certainly, Rance seemed content with his home and Cate considered it charming and cozy.

But all Landon did was sit in an office.

Cate pouted. "I wanted you to see the baby. She is so utterly perfect."

"You realize you're bringing me further into your little scheme."

"I wish you wouldn't call it that."

"I wish you wouldn't lie to the rest of our family."

"I wish you would try to be more understanding."

Phoebe scoffed. "You believe this is my way of not being

understanding? Woe to you if I ever decided to stop under-standing the utterly nonsensical situation you've gotten yourself into. You would have not a single ally to help make your story sound legitimate. You would be in this on your own and would have no one to talk to. Or to help you put together the list of items Landon needs to make the house look like you live there."

"Thank you for that."

She huffed, both incensed and knowing there was nothing to be done about it. "You're welcome."

They walked past the last stately home before reaching Landon's, and Phoebe made a sort of strangled noise when she took in its beauty. "My heavens. He lives here?"

Cate felt the slightest twinge of pride when she nodded. "An architect from San Francisco designed it. A friend of the family, supposedly. He left nothing out."

He had not, indeed. The house had been designed in the Italianate style, the outer walls a pale yellow while the hand-carved wood trim was snow-white. The east side of the house featured a porch running from one end to the other, along with a balcony situated above the more modest front porch and accessible by double doors at the end of the upstairs hall.

"This is a mansion, not merely a house," Phoebe breathed. "You said his father is a senator?"

"Yes, and he does something-or-other with business. I truly know little about that."

"Well, he has enough to promise an unnamed sum for the building of your theater. I suppose that makes him quite wealthy, indeed." Phoebe giggled as they ascended the sandstone stairs. "I never would have imagined you being the one to land the wealthiest husband."

"And why not?" Cate sniffed. "I'm hardly hideous, you know."

Phoebe looked around upon entering, her eyes just as wide as they'd been upon first taking in the house's exterior. "Perhaps you can make this man fall in love with you and remain married," she suggested in a solemn whisper, as if they were in church.

"How could you even suggest such a thing?" Cate scolded as she removed her coat and hat. "You, of all people. The one who's always believed in romance."

"There is something romantic about falling in love with a man after you've married him," she reasoned, going from room to room.

Landon was at his office, and the two of them had said their goodbyes for the time being before Cate left to fetch Phoebe and bring her back to show off the baby.

And the house. She couldn't help herself. It was truly grand.

Mrs. Davis was in the kitchen, jumping in surprise when Cate entered.

"Forgive me." Cate chuckled. "I merely wished to bring my sister by to see Violet before I take her to the ranch. I, ah, trust Mr. Jenkins has explained the situation."

"He has, at that." Mrs. Davis settled her large body into a chair with a sigh, pulling a cup of tea closer. "Oh, my knees. I've been up and down the stairs so many times. Not that I'm complaining, mind you, but it is quite a change for a woman of my advanced years. Suddenly caring for an infant when my children have children of their own. I haven't the energy any longer, and that's a fact."

"I'm sure I can't imagine. You'll have a few days to breathe now."

"I will at that, and I thank you for it. Though I must say, I shall miss the sweet little thing."

"Is she sleeping upstairs?" Cate asked.

Mrs. Davis nodded.

She pulled Phoebe down the hall and up the stairs, eager to show Violet off.

"Are you sure you have it in you to care for such a young baby?" Phoebe whispered, her voice heavy with doubt.

"I can do anything I decide to do. You ought to know that by now." In reality, Cate practically quaked with apprehension. Who was she to think she knew better than a grandmother how to raise a baby? She'd never done more than play with Edward, and he was so much older. He did not require the same sort of attention.

At the moment, though, it was easy to fall in love with the notion of it. When the baby was sleeping, quiet, and all was still and sweet. Cate tiptoed to the basket, left on the floor at the foot of the bed.

"The wife's room?" Phoebe asked on entering. "I suppose you'll sleep here."

"I suppose so," Cate shrugged before bending to lift the sleeping baby. She squirmed a bit before opening her eyes and looking up at her visitors.

She'd only been beautiful and perfect before, while sleeping.

Now? With wide, solemn blue eyes that looked up into Cate's? She was an angel sent from heaven.

"Oh, my," Phoebe breathed, smiling from ear to ear. "She certainly is a beauty, isn't she? Sweet Violet. What a lovely little girl you are."

"I told you," Cate whispered, rocking the baby in her arms. "Isn't she lovely? I can't imagine how anyone could consider her a burden. I truly cannot."

"You might feel differently when she's crying."

"I doubt it."

At that moment, as if she understood, Violet decided to test Cate's patience. Her small, rosebud mouth opened as if she intended to yawn. Then, instead of yawning sweetly, she let out an ear-piercing wail that set Cate's teeth on edge.

"She certainly can scream!" Cate laughed, though it was an empty laugh. A laugh tinged with dismay. Was this what Landon had been going on about?

"Walk her around!" Phoebe suggested, wringing her hands as Cate moved around the room. "Bounce her a little!"

"Bounce her?"

"You know." Phoebe moved up and down on the balls of her feet. "Gently. Move her about."

Cate did her best, but it was to no avail. Violet screamed until the color of her skin matched her name.

"Shh, darling. It's all right. Everything is well. You'll be all right."

"Is she in need of a changing?" Phoebe suggested, and she stepped aside as Cate laid Violet on the bed and lifted up her gown to check. Yes, her cloth diaper was soiled.

They searched the room for clean cloth while Violet continued to wail. Cate imagined she would tire herself out eventually, but it seemed that wasn't so. She simply drew in a lungful of air and screamed again.

"For heaven's sake," Cate scolded in a whisper as she changed the baby. "One would think you were on fire, the way you carry on. That is no way for a young lady to behave. Has anyone ever told you that?"

Once finished, she lifted Violet into her arms. "Perhaps we'd better find out from Mrs. Davis what her feeding schedule is. She might be hungry. And I ought to be on my way with her soon."

Phoebe looked skeptical, to say the least. "Are you certain this is the right course of action?"

"Naturally. Listen, she's barely making a sound now." Indeed, her screams had quieted to little more than pitiful whimpers, her tiny face scrunched up. "I'm sure she's only hungry. Otherwise, she has no fever and seems to be in good health. Once she eats, she'll settle down."

Phoebe still frowned as she turned and left the room—fled was more like it. Cate supposed she was glad to be away from the little one for a while.

Now that they were alone, Cate looked down at her. "I have to admit, I have no idea what I'm doing," she whispered, sitting because her knees suddenly felt shaky. "I need you to agree to meet me halfway, darling. Because if we're going to make this work, we have to work together. That means behaving yourself and allowing me to take care of you. Otherwise, I'm afraid my sisters will be awfully upset with both of us."

Violet let out a tiny cry and kicked out with both legs.

"All right, they will be awfully upset with me," Cate sighed. "It isn't your fault. They'll be upset with me. I'm only trying to do the right thing. Why does it seem that whenever I try to do the right thing, I get myself into trouble?"

And this time, she'd pulled a baby into it with her. A baby who could very well wail throughout the drive to the ranch and throughout the duration of their time there.

"If there was a way to avoid taking you, I would, but I feel your father needs the time to get himself in order before your grandparents come. And it would do well for us to at least appear as mother and daughter, would it not? By the time they arrive, we'll have to make it look like we've been together all your life. I am an actress, but I don't know if even I'm good enough to fool them."

She took Violet's hand, the tiny fingers and their tiny nails looking all the smaller next to her own. "I suppose we're in this together. At least I have one friend."

A friend who could only communicate by crying.

It was going to be a long week, indeed.

9

———

She would be leaving soon, if she had not left already.

Landon's gaze shifted toward the window, where he'd found himself gazing throughout the day. Good thing Mr. Witherspoon hadn't caught him doing it.

He could hardly look at the bank president without remembering his disparaging attitude toward Cate when she'd entered the bank. How brave she'd been to even consider such a thing, yet the man had treated the entire event as a joke.

At least he'd been on his way out of the bank for the day by the time it had all transpired, and there hadn't been a need to face Witherspoon again until the following morning when his anger had cooled somewhat.

"Landon." Bill Jones waved a hand from just inside his office doorway. "Is there something wrong with your hearing?"

"No, no, of course not." He straightened himself out and sat upright, the way a bank's vice-president was supposed to.

"I've been calling out to you," Bill informed him with a good-natured wink. "Too much carousing last night?"

Carousing. Hardly. What he wouldn't give at times for the opportunity to carouse. Those days were already in the past, unattainable. The man he'd once been.

Bill was unaware of this. While the two of them had become good friends in the five years since Landon's arrival in Carson City upon accepting the bank position, Landon didn't feel he could even confide in perhaps the one person who would understand best.

While Bill had never found himself in this position—to Landon's knowledge—he'd known his share of encounters with obliging young women and in fact seemed to make a sport of convincing them to give into his wiles.

There were times when Landon thought his favorite part was sitting down to recount these adventures over a whiskey and a cigar at the saloon, or even sometimes in one of their offices.

But this? This was an entirely different matter, and no one could be trusted. What would Witherspoon think if he knew Landon had fathered a child and now scrambled like a madman to provide proper care for the infant? What would any of them think? What would they whisper behind their hands when he strolled Carson Street?

How would it affect his position at the bank?

And how long would it take to reach his father?

He'd consoled himself many times over with the knowledge that he no longer had to rely on his family's wealth. Oliver Jenkins might have insisted on that Italianate mansion for no Jenkins could live in anything less impressive, but that had been the extent of the assistance Landon would accept.

Even if his father threatened to disown him and cut him out of any inheritance, he had more than enough set aside to live comfortably the rest of his days. He could even repay the costs of the house if called upon to do so.

Of course, that would leave Cate without the money for her theater.

Perhaps he'd spoken too soon, offering her the money as he'd done.

Bill waited for him to answer. He managed a smile. "Something of that nature."

Bill's eyes lit up, as they normally did when the subject turned to women. "Well? Who was she? That Ida of yours? I told you she'd wait for you to return."

Ida. Yes, she'd been waiting for him to return, all right. She'd wasted no time arriving at his doorstep, and he could not blame her in the least. "No, another one. You don't know her. We only recently met."

"In the week since you returned? I should've known." Bill winked before entering the office and taking a seat at one of the two chairs before Landon's desk.

"No, it isn't like that."

"Oh, isn't it? Then I haven't known you for all these years."

Landon reminded himself that he was speaking to the president's nephew. He then reminded himself that for all his faults, Bill was not a bad person. He had no way of knowing the strain Landon had been under.

Or that Landon was referring to his infant daughter and not a young woman from town. The thought of Violet sent him looking out the window again, as if he would catch sight of her.

"Are you waiting for something to happen?" Bill asked. "I can't help but be concerned when you won't stop looking out the window that way. As if you expect an explosion."

Landon laughed genuinely this time. "Hardly. I admit, I'm distracted, but it isn't anything so terribly serious."

"I'm glad to hear that, as I have an important engagement this evening and would hate to be injured in a blast."

Landon's brows lifted. "Oh? What sort of engagement?"

"I'll give you three guesses." Bill leaned back in the chair, crossing ankle over knee. He was, on the surface, the perfect gentleman. A blue blood from back East whose father had followed the wave of Easterners seeking fortune along the Transcontinental Railroad.

Beneath the polished surface, the education, the fine taste in clothing and impeccable manners, he was a man who lived by his appetites and did not believe in denying himself.

In fact, he indulged whenever possible. How he'd never gotten himself into a situation such as Landon's was a mystery.

"I hope you enjoy yourself."

"I hope you do, as well, since I need you to join us."

"What? Why me?"

"You see, she has a sister..."

Landon rolled his eyes. "I should've known."

"All you need do is join us at the restaurant and enjoy the evening. I'm sure the young woman is nice company."

"Then why is she accompanying her sister rather than stepping out with a suitor of her own?"

"She's quite shy."

"Regardless of the reason why the young woman cannot find a suitor to take her to supper, I'm afraid I cannot join you."

Bill's face fell. "Why not? You owe me from the last time I joined you in a situation like this."

"Over a year ago."

"And?"

Landon laughed. "I have other things to do tonight."

"Such as?"

"Such as personal matters that need attending to. Which are none of your business," he added when Bill opened his mouth to ask.

"What will I do now? I cannot take this woman to supper without her sister in tow."

"I've never heard you complain about being in the company of two women at once."

"This is hardly the same situation."

"Because you wanted to push one of them off on me."

Bill's head shook mournfully as he left. "You make it sound so unpleasant."

Life had changed such a great deal in such a short amount of time. He was now a man with responsibilities, and as his wife had reminded him, he needed to start thinking as a married man would.

He also needed to purchase the items on her list, which meant visiting the general store and making a spectacle of himself. What would the store's clerks think of his sudden interest in setting up house?

He told himself it did not matter, especially if it made his wife happy and comfortable. His wife! What would Bill think? How hard would he laugh if he had the first idea what Landon had been up to?

At least there was one item he would not have to purchase. He'd forgotten about its existence until after he'd left for the bank. His mother had given it to him on his last visit to his childhood home, and while he'd protested the gift at the time, he was now infinitely relieved that she'd insisted he take it.

"Just in case," Hermione had winked while slipping the gold band into his pocket. A gold band set with a pearl, flanked by a pair of small rubies.

He'd give it to Cate when she returned to play the part of happy, doting wife. It would make his mother so happy, and she needed all the happiness available to her.

This was hardly the way he'd imagined giving that ring to a woman, but it was all for a good cause.

Once his parents were out of town, he could find a way to settle the situation to his liking. He would find a governess or some such woman to care for the baby while he worked, and life could return somewhat to normal. There were three spare bedrooms in the home, as Mrs. Davis did not live under his roof—with only himself to care for, there was little need for her to do more than report in the morning and go home after his supper had been seen to.

Yes, this would all work out. So long as his parents left on schedule and allowed him the privacy he craved, and the time he needed to create an actual life for his daughter. She deserved that much, at least, after starting out the way she had.

And so long as Cate was the actress she made herself out to be. That remained to be seen.

If anyone had ever told him he'd stake his future and his parents' happiness on a girl with the sorts of strange notions she entertained, he would have laughed himself sick.

10

Only once had she experienced such apprehension upon approaching the ranch and its sprawling house. At the time, she'd not known what she and her sisters were headed for, and any number of unsavory scenarios had raced through her head as the wagon carrying the family had approached for the first time since their early childhood.

This was hardly the first time she'd watched the house come into view as she came to the end of a long drive from town. By now, she practically knew each piece of the land by heart. She knew what to expect from it, its dips and turns, the areas to avoid.

She did not, however, know what to expect from her sisters upon coming to a stop in front of the porch.

"That isn't quite true, either," she admitted to Violet, who slept beneath a pile of blankets near her feet. It was warm and cozy down there, with a hot brick nearby to add extra comfort and safety.

Amazing, all the things one needed to consider when traveling out-of-doors with a baby. She would never take her freedom for granted again. Nor the ability to think of only herself and her comfort and safety.

No, it was not quite true that she did not know what to expect from her sisters. In fact, she could predict exactly how the event would unfold.

Molly would demand to know why an infant suddenly arrived at their doorstep and might even listen with sympathy as Cate told a tale of woe regarding a friend who had suddenly developed sweating fevers and a heavy cough. A friend who feared for her child's health, who also had neither the strength nor the means to provide care while in such a condition.

What a dramatic tale she would tell, full of emotion. Perhaps this friend of hers was on the verge of death.

Molly was a practical person. She would see the necessity of sending a child elsewhere when one was so ill. Near death, even.

What she would not understand, however, was why the task of caring for this infant had fallen upon Cate's shoulders.

No matter how many times she'd assure Molly that she need not interrupt her life in the slightest, that Cate had every intention of taking the child's care into her own more than capable hands, Molly would refuse to listen. Just as she normally refused to listen to reason when it came from her youngest sister.

She would simply have to bear it, just as she bore all of the little indignities and slights to which she was routinely subjected.

"All right, little baby." Cate drew the team to a halt, her heart racing to the point where she felt ill. It was now or never. To her credit, Violet had slept through much of the ride. For a moment, Cate considered taking the team out for a drive at night when the baby couldn't sleep. Perhaps that would help her—along with helping the inhabitants of the house, who would undoubtedly hear the baby's cries.

That was something that worried her greatly. She'd had no idea babies could scream so loudly, and that their screams could carry so far.

Surely, when she worked herself up into true fit, Violet's squalls would be audible from one end of the house to the other.

This would earn Cate little sympathy. In fact, it might earn her outright animosity, perhaps hostility.

Yet that was still preferable to being found out as having married Landon. Oh, the screaming that would follow such a discovery would put even Violet's most terrible fits to shame.

Lewis came from the stables, waving an arm over his head. He would come to unhitch the team, undoubtedly. She braced herself. This was the first test.

He was a reasonable man. Mild-mannered, intelligent. He had a good deal of sense, and often acted as a go-between for Molly and the rest of the girls. He tended to smooth her rough edges, to soften her sharp words. This was true more than ever now that she was with child and sometimes irritable and generally tired.

Cate favored him with her biggest smile while lifting the basket from inside the buggy and descending. "Before you ask," she called out, "this is only temporary. My friend is ill and cannot care for the baby at the moment. I offered to help."

Lewis came up short when he realized what she carried. "A baby?" he asked, his brows knitting together beneath the wide brim of his hat.

"Yes, a baby. See? This will be excellent practice for when your baby comes." She even managed to giggle, as if feeling playful and not at all as if she might lose the contents of her stomach at any moment.

"You brought a baby to the ranch without asking if anyone would object?"

There were limits to her patience, even when she knew how important it was to gain sympathy and an ally against what was surely to come. "You and Molly are going to have a baby, and you didn't think to ask if any of us objected."

He merely shook his head, smirking. "Oh, and I thought today would be a quiet day."

"It isn't going to be as bad as that," she assured him, hoping this was not a lie. "It will only be for a few days, until my friend is on the mend. She will send for the baby when she is well enough. For now, it didn't seem prudent to expose the child to such illness when she is so small." Cate dipped her hand into the basket and eased back the blanket which half-covered Violet's face. Her downy skin, so soft and smooth, her little rosebud mouth puckered as if she were deep in thought while dreaming sweet dreams.

That did it. She'd known it would. Under his tough exterior, Lewis had a tender heart. The corners of his mouth tugged upward.

"She's a pretty one," he admitted.

"And an angel," she lied. No sense in destroying his illusions too quickly. "I had better get her inside, as she is due to be fed shortly."

His head snapped up in surprise. "Do you have everything you need?"

"Of course, I made certain to bring along everything the baby needs. I've thought of everything."

The front door opened, and out came Holly with Edward on one hip. "What's taking so long? You ought to come inside out of the cold."

"If it's so cold, why did you come out?" Cate asked, laughing merrily. Best to keep spirits up, she knew. To keep the mood light and airy. "Lewis was just admiring my new friend, who I brought to stay with us for a few days while her mother recovers from illness."

Holly gasped loud enough to startle Edward, who immediately began to fret.

"You have nothing to fear," Cate assured him with a peck on his cheek. She held out the basket for them both to admire the baby. "See? You were once a baby like this, dear. So small and weak and helpless."

"You don't know the first thing about caring for a baby!" Holly reminded her, as if she needed reminding.

"Now, as I said it will only be a few days. I know how to feed her, how to change her, how to dress her and how to bathe her. What else is there to know?" She sailed into the house as if nothing bothered her in the least, though her heart continued to race madly, and her palms were slick with sweat. Perspiration even began to dampen the nape of her neck.

She was an actress, and this was her greatest role. She need only keep this in mind, and she resolved to do so as she turned to her sister with a wide smile. "Her name is Violet Jenkins, and she is an absolute angel. Just look at her."

She lowered the basket to the parlor floor before lifting Violet from her nest of blankets and holding her in the crook of one arm.

Holly came over to admire her, and Edward reached down to touch her hand.

"See, nothing to be afraid of. She can sleep in my room, and I will see to her feeding schedule. Which reminds me once again, she will need to be fed soon. She does not like to be kept waiting." That was an understatement if ever there was one, since Cate's ears still rang from the punishment they had received back at Landon's house.

She thought of him then, wondering how relieved he must be to have his house to himself again. She supposed a young, extremely eligible bachelor such as himself must regard sudden fatherhood as a terrible inconvenience.

Molly's footfalls echoed down the stairs, sending a new shot of terror through Cate's heart.

She began explaining before her sister even entered the room. "My friend is ill, and this will only be for a few days. Her name is Violet, and she is two months old and I know all there is to know about taking care of her, so you needn't—"

She stopped when it was clear Molly wasn't about to speak. She regarded Cate in silence, hands crossed over her swelling belly. She had ceased wearing her stays, and it was still a bit of shock to see her this way. Cate thought she secretly enjoyed not having to squeeze herself into the unforgiving device every day. Neither of them had ever taken to wearing the thing overnight. It was impossible to sleep comfortably when one could not draw a deep breath.

"I did not ask you to explain, and I have no argument to offer." Molly's mild tone was somehow more disturbing than it would have been had she shouted and screamed and stomped her feet.

Cate eyed her, suspicious. "Do you mean that?"

"Yes, I do. It simply isn't worth the strain. Dr. Perkins tells me I ought to keep myself calm as I can, and I've promised Lewis I would do my best. Therefore I can only say welcome to this child and that I hope you know what you're getting yourself into."

How she managed to deliver a stinging blow without so much as raising her voice was a mystery.

Cate made a mental note of this, of how a menacingly low tone of voice could be far more powerful than one raised in a mighty roar. This would surely help her one day when she was on stage.

In her theater.

This reminder bolstered her, giving her added strength with which she might stand up to her imperious sister. "I'm glad of this. The doctor knows best."

"Yes, and I should have known you would find a way to challenge me."

"Now, now." Holly stepped in between them. "It isn't so bad is that. I would hate to see anything befall this sweet angel while her mother is ill. Cate's heart, as always, is in the right place. She only wants to be of help."

Molly rolled her eyes. "No. Cate's heart, as always, got in the way of her head. Sometimes I wonder if you think at all. Do you?"

This stung, and there was no hope of hiding the fact.

"One day, you will come to know how you have under-estimated me. And you will apologize for having done so. You have never given me the credit I deserve."

"Perhaps if you did anything to earn that credit, I would give it to you. Anyone who knows me knows I'm a fair person, but you seem determined to push me to the limit at every turn."

"Well, worry not. Perhaps the time will come sooner than you think that I will no longer be a problem for you. You won't have to worry about me ever again." She returned the baby to the basket and carried it, along with the baby's things, upstairs to her room.

She might have stomped her feet a bit louder than was

necessary along the way, but she needed to find some way to express her outrage.

"If you plan to care for a child, perhaps you had best stop behaving like a child yourself!" Molly called up after her.

Cate responded by slamming her bedroom door as hard as she possibly could manage.

Only once the deed was done did she see the folly in it.

Violet was startled from her sleep and began to wail.

Cate closed her eyes, leaning against the door and asking once again what she had gotten herself into.

11

Incredible, really, what a good night's sleep could do.

Landon awoke that morning feeling like a new man. A quick glance at the pocket watch he'd left on his bedside table—a gift upon his graduation from Harvard—told him he'd slept nearly eleven straight hours.

This was hardly his customary schedule, but he'd needed it a great deal.

He had even refused his supper the night before, choosing instead to soak in a scalding tub instead. He'd silently thanked his father's architect friend all the while for insisting on installing plumbing indoors, hot and cold water included.

Normally, he would have been dining alone, or preparing to join Bill or another friend somewhere in town. Instead, he'd collapsed into bed at seven o'clock and had slept straight through.

Was this the way of it for all mothers and fathers?

Suddenly, sleep was more important than anything else in life. He'd had no time in which to prepare himself, rather than having the customary nine months most fathers were granted in which he might ease himself into the situation.

One single night's sleep had been enough to turn things around. Now, he was ravenously hungry and eager to start his day.

Until he passed the closed door of the next bedroom over, that was. It was surprising, the way his heart sank just a bit when he remembered there was no one behind that door.

As greatly as she shaken his entire life, he missed her. He had to remind himself that she would be home in a few days, that he might have the chance to enjoy her then. It would be easier to do so while Cate and his parents were there, as well. He would especially enjoy watching his mother interact with her granddaughter.

He supposed that was the way that for most fathers, too.

Mrs. Davis had not yet arrived for the morning, but it was no bother. She needed the rest just as badly as he did. Perhaps more; after all, she was more than twice his age. He brewed coffee and fixed himself a simple breakfast of fried eggs and biscuits left over from the night before, slathered with butter and preserves. A shame he'd not eaten them for supper, for they must have been quite delicious when fresh out of the oven. As it was, they did quite well the morning after.

The items he had purchased at the general store were to be delivered early in the afternoon, and he made a point of leaving a note for Mrs. Davis to explain this in case he were to miss her on his way to the bank. He then hurried through his morning's grooming and found himself whistling as he shaved.

Life was truly looking up. For the first time in over a week, he had help. Cate would return, they would have time to get to know each other and to arrange the house to her liking before his parents arrived.

He had the utmost faith in her. She was a sharp girl, fast on her feet, and she would certainly adapt to his life nicely. He had nothing to worry about, for she would see this as her greatest acting role. Though he did not know her well, he knew that much.

He had always been an excellent judge of character, after all. One of the many instincts which aided him in business. It was important for a man in his position to quickly and accurately sum up strangers to whom he was about to make a business proposition.

At times, it became clear before he'd even started that he would be wasting his time, that he would not wish to do business with the person in question. Knowing the difference between a good partner and a bad partner was just as important as being able to convince a good partner the benefits of said partnership.

He decided to break out a suit of clothes which he purchased in Chicago but had not yet had a chance to enjoy. Rather than a traditional sack coat, the tailor had referred to this as a frockcoat—shorter, better fitted, with narrower lapels. The matching waistcoat had no lapels, which he had been assured was the new fashion in Paris and New York.

Landon hardly considered himself fashionable, but he did wish to make a good impression once his parents arrived. His mother and father would wish to see him looking his best, which meant making use of the wardrobe he purchased during his travels. He'd better get accustomed to dressing the part.

It only occurred to him then that Cate might not possess the clothing of a wife of a man in his position. He met his eyes in the looking glass above the basin, some of his good mood now darkening.

No, she was a fine young lady, raised in the East. She would know how to dress, how to groom, how to conduct herself. He wished they had more time to discuss what she ought to bring back from the ranch and wondered if the dressmaker would be able to help should she be in need of anything at the last minute.

Just another opportunity for him to exercise a bit of faith. He would need to call all of his faith into service over the next week.

And then it would be over. He could return to wondering what to do with his life now that he had a child. And Cate could have her theater.

The house was still quiet when he slid his arms into the sleeves of his topcoat, its fur-lined collar a necessity against the bitter cold air. He hoped Cate had bundled Violet up appropriately and wondered if he would ever stop worrying about the child. He supposed not. He supposed that the tiny stranger would grow into a girl, then a young lady.

And he might just wish for the days when he had nothing more to worry about than whether or not she would allow him to sleep through the night.

He was smiling to himself as he entered the bank, nodding and greeting to the clerks he passed along the way to his office. "Good morning, Mr. Witherspoon," he called out as he passed, not waiting for the man to reply before he entered the solitude of his office.

One of the boys whose task it was to run errands and see to the needs of the bank officers followed behind, accepting his topcoat and hat. "Pardon me, sir, but a telegram was discovered this morning among other messages which arrived yesterday afternoon. It fell to the floor, beneath the desk of one of the clerks. I found this morning and placed it on your desk."

Landon smiled to himself, interpreting the boy's explanation for what it was. He expected praise for doing what should have been done the previous afternoon.

"I only hope it was nothing urgent," he muttered. "In the future, if any such occasion should arise, see to it the message is brought to my home rather than left here. Do you understand?"

The boy's face reddened until his freckles disappeared. "Of course, sir. I'm sorry."

He was shaking his head as he opened the envelope, his good mood dissolving by the moment. It seemed there were times when the rest of the world was determined to make his life more difficult.

Never had that seemed more the case that at that moment, as he stared down at the slip of paper which had been sent around dinner time the previous day.

Meetings canceled. Mother anxious to see you. Will arrive tomorrow evening.

No.

It couldn't be true.

Landon read and reread the short message, certain he must be misunderstanding. It surely did not say his parents would be arriving that very evening. Such a thing was impossible.

He stormed out of his office, clutching the telegram in one shaking hand. "Why was I not given this yesterday?" he called out, expecting no answer but needing to voice his disapproval, nonetheless.

"What's this all about?" Bill asked, coming from his own office. "Is it bad news?"

"It depends upon what you consider bad news." He thrust the telegram toward his friend while his mind raced sickeningly from one thought to the next. The house wasn't ready. Cate was at the ranch. They hadn't the time to get to know each other better. It would be clear from the start they were strangers.

Bill winced. "Nothing will chill a man's blood like the prospect of a family visit." He chuckled.

"I'm glad you find this amusing." Landon returned to

his office, running his hands through his hair until it stood on end.

Bill followed. "What is it, old man? I don't think I've ever seen you so undone."

"I wish I could explain, but it would take far too much time and time is a luxury I do not have at present." He had to think. He had to plan. If only he knew exactly when they would arrive that evening.

It was barely eight o'clock in the morning. He had time, didn't he? He could make a success of this still.

Tearing sheet from the blotter on his desk, he scrawled a quick note. *You must return at once. Parents are arriving this evening, just received word this morning. Please hurry.*

Folding the note, he marched from his office once again. "I need someone to deliver a message for me," he announced.

One of the errand boys seated closest to the door leapt to his feet. Landon recognized him as one always eager to be of service.

"I would be happy to help, sir," he assured him.

Landon sized him up. Young, but likely trustworthy. He would want to impress, which meant he would take great pains to deliver the message successfully.

He pulled the boy aside, reaching for the billfold in the inside pocket of his waistcoat. "Do you know how to find the Reed Ranch?" He asked.

"Yes, Sir. It lies due west of town, perhaps one to two hours ride depending on the speed of one's horse."

Landon was impressed, in spite of the panic rising in

his throat. The lad would go far if he showed this much intelligence and thoroughness in other areas of his life.

"Fine, fine. I need you to take this note to Miss Cate Reed. Do you understand? It is to be read by her and her alone. Not by you, not by one of her sisters or the ranch hands. Do you understand?"

The boy nodded, Adam's apple bobbing in his thin throat when he swallowed. "Yes. Yes, sir. I understand."

"That's fine. Here is a dollar for your trouble, and there will be another waiting for you when you return. You must make haste. Miss Reed must receive this note at the earliest opportunity. Do you understand?"

"Of course. You can count on me, sir." If the boy had saluted, Landon would not have been the least bit surprised.

He sent him on his way, hoping against hope the boy was as trustworthy as he seemed. There was nothing to do but trust, and then do his best to control what he could.

He went to Witherspoon's office next, finding the old man smoking one of his customary cigars while reading papers on his desk. By the end of the day, the entire room would be shrouded in a fog of smoke. "Sir, I'm afraid I've just been made aware of an urgent situation."

Witherspoon glanced up, frowning. "Anything I can do, my boy?"

How Landon hated when he regarded him this way, treating him as if he saw himself as a father figure. Landon knew that, bank president or not, the old man saw potential in Landon's family connections more so than he did in Landon himself.

"You might allow me the rest of the day away from the bank, sir. You know I would never ask, but I only just received a telegram from my father this morning which he sent yesterday afternoon. For some reason, it was delivered here to the bank and not to my home, and I didn't have a chance to look at it until today. He and my mother are arriving this evening, though he did not give me a firm time. I must see to the arrangement of household, as they will be staying with me during their visit."

Witherspoon's eyes lit up, and Landon knew he saw opportunity in this. He would likely seek to ingratiate himself with a senator.

His father would not be impressed, but Witherspoon did not need to know this. So long as he was willing to grant the day off, it would not hurt for him to believe he might curry favor with the great Oliver Jenkins.

"Of course, my boy! You must see to your parents' comfort. I take it their arrival is a bit of a surprise."

Landon pulled a face, nodding. "They were not supposed to arrive for another five days. He said something about canceled meetings."

Witherspoon laughed merrily, as if this were a tremendous joke and nothing was amiss. Naturally, he was unaware of anything being amiss, and both he and Bill could see the situation from a humorous perspective. Landon supposed he would feel the same, were it Bill in his shoes, with him unknowing of the true nature of the situation.

"Thank you, sir. I can assure you this will not affect—"

"Say nothing of it, Landon. If you need time away from the bank during their visit, I am happy to oblige. After all, you took a great deal of time away from home this last year, and the least I can do to thank you for representing us in such a fine manner is to grant you time to visit with your loving parents."

Landon decided to leave before the man began kissing his feet. "Thank you, sir. I will be sure to mention to my father how generous you've been."

That would seal things, and Mr. Witherspoon would go to bed happy man that night.

With that problem solved, and the note on its way to the ranch, Landon gathered his things and put out the desk lamp. There was so much to do. Mrs. Davis would be in a tizzy, and he could only hope that Cate might arrive before his parents did.

Otherwise, his scheme would be over before it began.

12

"Hush, dear," Cate murmured, walking back and forth yet again with Violet against her shoulder. She patted her back gently yet firmly, determined to bring up whatever it was that caused the baby such distress. "You must rid yourself of that nasty bubble, my dear. It will hurt your little belly if you do not." She went so far as to bounce her gently up and down, hoping to encourage the air to expel itself through her mouth.

She was so tired. She could not remember a time when she had ever been this tired.

It seemed there was always something to do. Feeding, washing the bottle, preparing a new bottle. Making certain there was enough milk available, which there normally was. Their cows produced a great quantity, yet what the baby did not drink immediately had to be chilled to keep it fresh, which meant ensuring there was enough chilled milk on hand.

She soiled her diapers nearly constantly, requiring repeated changing before the washing of the soiled diapers.

Then there was the walking. The constant walking. If she'd been worn a groove in the embroidered rug which decorated her bedroom floor, it would not come as a surprise. She must have walked miles in service of keeping Violet happy and as quiet as could be.

And still, the baby had cried. Not nearly as loudly as she had at Landon's, but she made it a point to express her displeasure often and with great force. How a small baby could manage to be so loud was beyond human under-standing.

She caught a glimpse of herself in the looking glass above her dressing table and could barely recognize the girl there. Her hair hung in snarls about her face, reminders of how Violet had grabbed it by the handful and pulled when she was in a particularly angry mood.

The circles beneath her eyes were pronounced, evidence of the mere minutes of sleep she had managed.

The baby's spit-up had dried on her shirtwaist in three places—she simply had not the time to change, and after the second incident had decided there was little point in changing. Why soil another shirtwaist, which Violet would invariably do the moment she changed from dirty to clean?

"Violet, please. Please sleep. I need to sleep, too." Her footsteps were slower than ever, yet she continued to pat the baby's back until a nearly violent belch erupted from her lips.

She winced, certain she would feel a rush of warmth down her back, no such sensation occurred. She looked to the baby, who now appeared to smile as she rested her head on Cate's shoulder. Now that she was comfortable, she might take a nap.

Cate could have wept with joy.

Holly and Molly had made it a point to stay away, which she might have resented were she not so thoroughly exhausted. Then again, Molly would only have reminded her what a terrible idea this was, to begin with, and Cate had no desire to be reminded. She understood all too well on her own.

Only the image of a theater which she carried in her mind was enough to remind her chin up. She could do this. She had to.

She lowered Violet into her basket and offered up a silent prayer of fervent thanks. Now she understood what it meant to be really and truly exhausted, one more experience she could add to future characters she would play. She would call upon this someday when portraying a character who'd been through more than she believed herself capable of, who then emerged on the other side victorious.

She was deep in thought about this as she changed her shirtwaist, even going so far as to imagine the audience before her, when the sound of voices raised in argument on the first floor got her attention.

She was only just finishing the top buttons, and she flew down the stairs.

"The baby is sleeping!" she hissed, prepared to claw to pieces anyone who disturbed her.

Roan looked at her, then pointed to the young man standing on the porch. "This boy says he has a message for you from a man in town," he muttered.

It was clear Roan distrusted the stranger, but then again, he distrusted most strangers. He had spent far too much of his life living alone.

The boy, for his part, looked positively prepared to die of fright. "From Mr. Jenkins," he managed to say through chattering teeth. He held out a folded slip of paper, his hand trembling slightly.

Of course. This would have to happen this way, would it not? She accepted the note, looking to Roan. "It is all right," she said. "He is only delivering a message."

With that, she turned to the poor boy who looked as though he had not yet begun to shave. So young, and so frightened. "Thank you very much. I'm sure Mr. Jenkins will be pleased to know you have delivered the message. Would you like something warm to drink before you start back to town?"

The boy's head shook violently as he backed away. "No, thank you," he whispered, glancing toward Roan and clearly frightened to death. He mounted his horse before hurrying away at a full gallop, dust rising in clouds behind him.

"Did you need to frighten the boy so?" she asked,

clicking her tongue and shaking her head as she unfolded the paper.

"I don't appreciate young boys speaking to me in such a dismissive manner," he muttered. "I don't care who this Mr. Jenkins is, though I do question how you know a man from town intimately enough that he is sending you messages this way."

Cate barely heard this, for the blood now rushed in her ears until nearly every other sound was drowned out.

She had to go back. Already? How could she manage it? She had only told the girls the day before that her friend was ill. How could she convince them the illness had turned around so quickly?

The paper shook so hard that it eventually fell to the floor, and Roan was quicker than she in bending to pick it up.

"What does this mean?" he asked after skimming the message.

Her cheeks flushed painfully hot as she grabbed the paper from him. "That is a private message."

"It isn't anymore. What does it mean? Who is this man, and why does he tell you to hurry to him? What have you been doing that you haven't told your sisters about?"

She held a finger to her lips, looking around. Molly was upstairs resting, while Holly had gone visiting at one of the neighboring ranches. The Beltons had just welcomed their second child, and Holly had wished to deliver a freshly baked cake has a congratulatory gift.

"Come with me," she whispered before taking the stairs

two at a time. It appeared as though any hope of resting should be forgotten, as she had a great deal to do now in a very short amount of time.

"What is this all about?" Roan whispered as she pushed him into her bedroom and closed the door as quietly as she could behind her. She noticed how uncomfortable he looked, being in her room, but there was little time for modesty at the moment.

"I need you to promise me you will not breathe a word of this." Throwing open the doors of her chifforobe, she studied her array of gowns, shirtwaists, and skirts, wondering what she ought to bring. He had not even given her a definite length of time in which his parents would visit. Three days? Four? She decided to be on the safe side and bring as much as her bags would hold.

"Not breathe a word of what?"

"What I'm about to tell you. Please, Roan, you must promise me. Phoebe knows of this too, and I had not intended to bring anyone else into my confidence, but it would appear as though there is no avoiding this."

"No avoiding what? You must tell me."

So, she did tell him, as she pulled one garment after another from the chifforobe and did what she could to arrange everything nicely, so it would not wrinkle terribly during the ride to town.

Roan averted his eyes when it came time to arrange her stockings, shifts, and petticoats.

"You see, there was nothing I could do. I wanted to help him, and to help her. The poor thing was sleeping in bed with whichever stranger was in charge of her at the moment."

When she turned to him, she found him slack-jawed in amazement.

"You married this man?" he whispered, aghast.

"Yes, but that is hardly the problem at hand just now. His parents are coming today, when they were not supposed to be here for another several days. I do not know him. I have to pretend to be his wife when I do not even know the man."

"But you are his wife."

"You know what I mean," she hissed. "Please, can you drive me and the baby to town? And not tell anyone, not even Holly?"

It was clear, she gave him great deal of pain, his brow wrinkling in distress at the thought of lying to his wife. "You're not really lying," she pointed out. "You are merely avoiding telling her the truth."

"Which is the same as lying."

"No, it isn't. Avoiding the truth is not the same as lying. And it is for a good cause, at any rate. This child is better cared for right now at this moment, than she has been her entire life, I would wager. And now, she will know the love of her grandparents and her father all at once. Is that not a good thing? I believe it is for the best."

"Cate…" he muttered, shaking his head. He was a man of honor, she knew, with very clear ideas of right and wrong. There was no in-between for a man like him.

She went to him, clasping his hands in hers and looking

straight in the eye. Hot, stinging tears threatened to spill over, but she did her best to fight them. "Please, Roan. You're the only one I can trust now. I need your help. I signed a contract, for heaven's sake! And do not tell me now whether you believe that to be a good idea or not, because the deed has been done. I must hold up my end of the contract, which means going to town and pretend to be Landon's wife and the mother of this child. No one is going to get hurt. If anything, I'm sparing this child a great deal of pain in the future. What will happen if her grandparents find out she is—"

"You needn't say it." There was a note of resignation his voice. She hated knowing she was the cause of it, but there was nothing to be done about that now. She would make it up to him in the future, just as she would make it up to Phoebe.

"Will you help me?" She searched his face for answers, knowing there was no time to waste but also knowing she needed his help, for someone would have to provide an explanation to the girls as to why she had suddenly disappeared.

It did pain her that it would have to be him, for he had never been anything but kind and understanding toward her, but these were desperate times.

"On one condition."

Who was she to protest? "What is it?"

"You allow me to meet this man. I want to know whose house you will be living in for the next several days. Do not try to get around me on this, for I will not allow you to do so. I will sit outside the house all night—"

She waved her hands, turning away to continue getting her things together. "Yes, yes. Fine. Whatever you want. Please, help me get these things downstairs?"

It seemed there were always new obstacles in her way, and no sooner did she think one problem was solved than two more popped up in its place.

She could only hope this would all end soon, and that she would have enough time to at least settle herself in before her mother and father-in-law arrived.

13

What was taking her so long?

He'd already been to the station and had learned that the train from California was set to arrive at six o'clock. That would give them several hours if she hurried. She simply had to hurry.

"Take that upstairs!" he shouted as a pair of men carried the crib through the front door. "The first room from the front!"

Mrs. Davis hurried about the place, dusting and arranging. "Did you purchase everything in the store? Is anything left for the rest of the town?"

He said nothing, choosing instead to pour himself a healthy glass of whiskey before downing it in one smooth, practiced flick of his wrist.

"Be careful not to drink to excess," the old woman reminded him before hurrying up the stairs to oversee the crib's placement. "It would not do for you to be inebriated—"

"I can manage myself, thank you very much!" he shouted after her, immediately feeling sorry for it. She simply did not know when to keep her thoughts to herself. As if he would allow himself to become inebriated on such an important day, with such important company on their way.

He merely needed something to steady his nerves.

It felt as I time was slipping away like water through his open fingers, simply pouring itself out. He suspected that where he was seated behind his desk, it would have gone much more slowly. That was usually the way of it. Just when he wanted time to slow down, it insisted on flowing away from him.

Perhaps the train would be late, and then he would have a bit more time with his new bride.

It was half-past-twelve according to his pocket watch. If the boy from the bank had delivered the note in a timely manner, she would by now have had the chance to gather her things and make her way from the ranch. He expected her arrival at any minute.

And he refused to give credence to the many ugly images which insisted on rising to the forefront of his mind. An accident along the way, perhaps, for either the boy or for Cate.

Obviously, if Cate had suffered an accident, there would be far greater consequences. His chest tightened painfully at the thought of his daughter being involved in anything of the sort, and his stomach turned against the whiskey he'd only just emptied into it. He felt as if his nerves were unraveling bit by bit, along with his sanity.

Everything he'd ordered had been delivered, at the very least. That was something to be grateful for. He paid both men who'd driven the cart from the general store a generous show of his appreciation, leaving the two of them smiling as if they'd just discovered gold. He supposed that to them, a dollar each was quite a princely sum.

He would have given them the entire contents of his billfold if it had meant bringing Cate and Violet to him that much sooner.

What did she expect to do with all this? That was what plagued him now as he stood, looking over the crates of goods which had been unceremoniously left in his downstairs hall. "Mrs. Davis!" he called out, tapping his foot impatiently.

"Yes, I am coming! Goodness gracious, I've never known such—"

He had no time for her complaints now. "I need you to help me make sense of why she asked for these things. She is not yet here to arrange them, and they need to be arranged before my parents arrive. Do you understand?"

The old woman merely sighed, wiping her hands on her apron. "There is not so much to setting up a house, I promise."

"You don't know. Look at all of this!" He waved his arm, indicating a dozen crates waiting to be unpacked. Already, the crib and rocking chair and other various items had been placed upstairs, but this? He was sure Cate had a scheme in mind, but he hadn't the first notion of exactly what it was.

Phoebe might know.

He turned to Mrs. Davis, hope beginning to glimmer in his mind. "Do you know where Sheriff Connelly lives?"

Mrs. Davis nodded. "In fact, he and his wife live only several houses away from myself."

What a stroke of luck. "Can you get there quickly? Please, ask for Mrs. Connelly. Take her aside and promptly explain that I need her help. Her sister has not yet arrived, and it is of the utmost importance that I have assistance while arranging the goods in the house. They must be taken care of before the train arrives at six o'clock."

She patted his shoulder before taking her time of fetching her coat from the hook in the front hall. He bit his tongue, grinding his teeth together to keep himself from telling her to hurry up.

She was a kind woman, patient, but he suspected she had her limit just as anyone else did. He needed all the allies he could get right now.

Alone, he went through the crates. Why did he need so many china figurines? So many bowls and vases? Lace squares and circles which he assumed might be meant for the arms of the sofa and chairs, but he could not be certain. There was an entire tea set, which made sense, though he did not know where she wished him to place it.

If only she had given him a list of where things ought to go, too.

Rather than wait, he bounded up the stairs and changed into a more appropriate suit rather than one he'd worn to the bank. He could barely button his waistcoat, his hands trembled so badly.

If only everything did not hang on this. If only he did not believe his parents would be grievously scandalized, and his mother's health worse than every should they learn the truth.

If only he had been smarter when it came to his dealings with Ida. If only he had restrained himself as a gentleman ought to.

He'd just finished changing into a more appropriate suit of clothes when the front door opened. How strange it was for him to hope to hear a baby's cry, but instead he heard two women talking rapidly. This would be Phoebe.

He ran downstairs to find a young woman who looked not unlike Cate standing, wide-eyed, looking over the crates.

"Mrs. Connelly?" he asked.

She nodded, unbuttoning her coat. "And I assume you're Mr. Jenkins, my brother-in-law. For the time being."

His skin crawled thanks to the discomfort her words caused. "Yes, that is true. Can you help me? I don't know when Cate will arrive, and my parents are coming sooner than expected—"

"Your housekeeper has already explained to me. Let us begin." Just like that, this efficient woman set about decorating his home as a wife would typically decorate it.

He followed her around, watching as she arranged

decorative bowls and vases, draping lace over the arms of nearly every piece of furniture on the first floor. The tea set sat in a place of honor on the table between the parlor's sofa and the two chairs opposite, all of this in front of the mantle which stretched along the outer wall.

"You might place those on the mantle," she suggested, pointing to a crate filled with odds and ends. A music box, a set of books whose titles he did not bother to read. An ornate lamp with a silk shade, cut glass droplets dangling from the braided edging.

He looked around and, with the room in better shape than it had been before, he recalled having seen such items in the parlors of his married friends. He'd simply never given much thought to it. Now, he understood the difference between what his home had looked like and what it needed to look like if one was to believe a woman lived there.

For even though he had more than enough money to see to his every need, he had developed a rather simple lifestyle at an early age thanks to his mother's impoverished background. While Oliver Jenkins had come from a great deal of money, Hermione had been orphaned at the age of eight and had gone to work to support her brothers and sisters immediately afterward.

It was her values, her beliefs which had shaped him much more so than those of his father. Yes, he had learned everything he knew about business from the man, but his mother had taught him how to live.

He set about clearing out the empty crates and the

excelsior which had been used to protect the items within once Phoebe had finished with them. "I don't know how to thank you," he said more than once.

"Yes, I know. My sister and I have already discussed that."

He looked her way, catching her in the act of eyeing him with suspicion. He could only imagine what she must think of him, and his shame was unspeakable.

Yet his pride and shame were of little concern at the moment. "Is there anything I can give you?"

She stared at him, standing in the center of his study after plumping the pillows on two wingback chairs. "Give me?"

Just when he thought he could not embarrass himself more. "Yes, that is, something for your trouble?"

She set her jaw at a determined angle, her chin jutting forward. "Mr. Jenkins. You might be accustomed to spending money quite freely, but it does not erase all debts. Do right by my sister, that is all I ask."

She humbled him. He hadn't the chance to express his regret for having chosen his words so foolishly before Cate floated through the front door with Violet in her basket.

"I came as fast as I could," she breathed.

He'd almost forgotten how fresh and young and lovely she was, how she seemed to brighten the room upon crossing the threshold. She was nothing less than a savior to him, and he could have lost control of his emotions with happiness at the sight of her.

Behind her was a tall man, his long hair held back by a

length of leather cord, and his face dark with what could only be anger as he glared at Landon.

"You coerced her into marriage?" the man demanded, storming into the house.

"Roan, please stop!" Cate hissed, clearly thinking of the baby.

Phoebe took the stranger by the arm. "This isn't necessary. The man has good intentions, and if anyone is to be blamed for all of this, it is our sister."

"She is only trying to help me." Landon stood his ground in front of the tall man, all but daring him to strike.

Landon would guarantee the man would come to regret it. For while Landon's business did not require much physical activity, he'd been a member of the boxing team at Harvard and would like nothing more in his current state of mind than to use his fists against a willing partner.

There was no need. "Roan, I am fully able to take care of myself. I make my own decisions. There was no coercion involved." Cate's tone was firm, leaving no room for argument. "Now, both you and my sister have seen my husband and my house for the time being with your own two eyes, and you know I am not in harm's way. I can manage from here. Thank you both very much."

"And just what do you think Molly and Holly will think when they find you gone?" Phoebe folded her arms, shaking her head at her younger sister. "Honestly, Cate, you don't think things through."

Cate's face turned an alarming shade of red, almost reminding Landon of Violet just before she was about to unleash a torrent of screams. He suspected that was exactly what he wished to do. She wished to scream at her sister, to rail against her belittling comments.

Instead, she smiled. "I still believe you shall be surprised. Both of you. If you'll excuse me, I must attend to the baby's welfare while preparing for the arrival of Mr. and Mrs. Jenkins. We can settle all of this once my time here at the house is complete."

Phoebe and Roan exchanged a look Landon could not understand, though their apprehension was clear.

Roan shrugged. "I suppose there's nothing else for us to do. She's made her bed, and it's time for her to lie in it."

For a moment, Landon felt terribly sorry for Cate. It was clear she was treated as the baby of the family. Granted, she had rather flighty ideas, and some of her stranger notions had left him struggling not to laugh. He could only imagine how many times her sisters had laughed at her over the years.

When he thought of that and recalled the way Mr. Witherspoon had dismissed her before hearing her out, he wished he could console her.

Roan cast one last disparaging look his way before affixing a wide-brimmed hat to his head and turning to leave. To think, Landon had imagined the sheriff and deputy being his most worrisome adversaries. He'd known nothing of this other brother-in-law.

Then again, he knew nothing of Cate's life whatsoever. And he had little time in which to learn.

She turned to him, her thoughts clearly following the same lines. "Well? Let us begin."

"I—I'm sorry to put you through this," he murmured, downcast after witnessing the dressing down she'd received thanks to him.

"It's nothing." She picked up the baby's basket from the floor, and he was pleased to find her looking happy and comfortable. There had been no reason to fear.

Cate had everything well in hand. She was far more capable than he'd given her credit for. Far stronger, too.

He told himself it was his responsibility to make these next few days as pleasant as he could for her. She deserved it.

"Yes," he agreed, and they climbed the stairs together. "Let's begin."

14

She'd thought a little pretending in front of her sister and brothers-in-law was the greatest performance of her life.

That had been nothing more than a dress rehearsal for this, the night she met her husband's parents for the first time.

Cate stepped away from the full-length looking glass, admiring her new evening dress. She'd had no chance to wear it before now. There was little reason to impress her sisters and brothers-in-law while dining at home.

It was hardly something she would have worn to the theater where she in Baltimore, but it was far too fine to be worn about the ranch at supper. Dark blue and black plaid, the tight bodice extended past her hips and blossomed into an impressive bustle at the back. The underskirt was of the same fabric, folded in the most exquisite, tiny pleats she'd ever seen.

She had brushed her hair until it shone, then arranged it in a series of curls and braids which she had expertly wound around the back of her head. A few loose tendrils floated free, brushing against the pleated neck of the bodice. A pair of pearl and diamond earbobs which had belonged to her mother danced and sparkled merrily when she turned her head from side to side.

At the very least, she did to her husband proud.

"May I come in?" The voice came from the door which separated her room from Landon's.

Her heart caught in her throat, for it wasn't until now that she truly understood how close they would be over the next several days. Only a thin wall and a door separated their bedchambers.

She hoped he would behave as a gentleman ought to.

"You may come in," she allowed. It was his house, after all.

She caught his reflection behind her own and noted the look of frank amazement on his face. He looked more handsome than ever, somehow, perhaps aided by the warm glow of the fire crackling away just beside him.

"You look lovely," he murmured. "I must admit, I had worried—"

She smirked. "You worried that I would not do you justice? That I would turn out to be nothing more than an inexperienced country girl?" She laughed when he flushed embarrassment. "Fear not. My mother raised ladies, and I'm certain she would spin in her grave if she knew what life turned out to be for us."

"They should be here shortly. It's half-past-five, the train is due to arrive at six. There is something I felt compelled to settle before they arrive."

She turned to him, expectant. "I've thought about this. It would be best for me to remain silent for a while. In fact, your father might regard me favorably if I held my tongue. This will help me avoid getting into any uncomfortable situations straightaway."

He nodded, distracted. "That is very wise of you, but it's not why I'm here. At the moment, I wish to give you this."

When he reached into the pocket of his waistcoat, she forgot to breathe. There was only one thing small enough to fit in there. One thing which would legitimize their entire arrangement.

He withdrew a gold band set with a single pearl, nestled between two sparkling rubies. She let out her breath in a slow, silent stream, transfixed by the ring's beauty.

"You see, when my parents met, my mother's family was not well-off at all. They lost their entire fortune just before my grandfather's passing. The only item my grandmother could not bring herself to sell that she might keep her children fed and clothed was this ring. It meant far too much to her to ever let go. She gave it to my mother, her oldest daughter, and my mother gave to me in the hopes that I would one day place it on the hand of my wife."

He'd been looking down at the ring as he delivered this speech, and only looked up at her once he finished. When he did, he grimaced.

"Did I upset you?" he asked, suddenly alarmed.

For she couldn't hold back the tears his story inspired, tears over the great suffering and sacrifice it must have taken to save that ring when it could have easily fed and housed a number of children for any number of days.

She could only imagine the love and devotion which the ring's owner had imbued it with, and now she would wear it upon her own finger.

For a moment, wrapped up in the romance of this notion, was a deep pang of guilt. The woman who wore this ring ought to have done so while in love. With a pure heart, with pure intentions. Not in the service of some elaborate lie.

Now, for the first time since they'd begun, she understood the enormity of what they were about to embark upon. She had to convince Mr. and Mrs. Jenkins that she was the sort of woman who could appreciate the beauty in this ring, that she deserved to wear it on her hand.

She was a good actress, but was she that good?

When she made no move to extend her hand, Landon took it and raised it on his own. He slid the cold band over her second to last finger, smiling.

"I had so hoped it would fit," he murmured with a soft laugh. "It would seem in keeping with our luck thus far if it didn't, would it not?"

She could not speak. She could hardly imagine anything to say that would do justice to this moment.

She'd just accepted a wedding ring from her husband, and yet she felt nothing for him but vague admiration and perhaps some inkling of attraction. He was a very handsome man, after all, and he had been very kind to her.

"Have I upset you? Is this too much?" Yes, he was a fine man, for he searched her face with true concern in his eyes and voice. Such blue eyes, too. He deserved a bride who would look up into them with nothing but the deepest love and devotion.

She was beginning to understand that she deserved eyes that would look down at her with nothing but the same. Not this sham of a marriage, which up to this point she had convinced herself was nothing more than a performance.

A single ring had brought everything to light in her heart. What a charlatan she was. Little wonder Phoebe and Roan were so cross with her.

"No," she murmured for his sake. "It isn't too much. It is just perfect. I'm glad you told me the story behind the ring, in case your mother mentions it."

He smiled, proud of himself. "Yes, I thought that was best. Now, I take my coffee black. I enjoy brandy after dinner, but I do not smoke cigars or a pipe, as I cannot stand the things."

She nodded, swallowing back the lump in her throat. Yes, she had to know about him. There was no time for sentiment. "Go on," she prompted.

"I attended Harvard University."

Her eyes widened in surprise. "My, you attended such a fine school?"

"Why not? It is one of the best schools in the country,

and my father believed I possessed an intellect requiring such education. I was on the boxing team there and earned several medals. I took the Grand Tour after graduation. I am an avid reader—I'm certain you have already seen the evidence of that in the library. I am my parents' only living child. Unfortunately, my mother suffered three stillbirths after I was born, and her health was never the same after the last."

Cate gasped, placing a hand over her breast. The poor woman. "She will be so happy to meet her granddaughter," she breathed.

He rewarded her with a genuine smile which seemed to stretch from ear to ear. "Yes, that is the one thought that has kept me steady throughout this entire thing. How happy she will be."

"And speaking of your daughter—"

Violet was happily engaged in opening and closing her tiny fists, staring at them as though they were the most fascinating things in the world.

Cate could not help but chuckle affectionately, in spite of the exhaustion which still plagued her, thanks to the little one.

"I hope she did not keep you up last night," Landon offered, standing at her side while the two of them looked down into the new crib. A lovely thing, brand-new, its wooden frame draped in the softest white lace.

Cate giggled. "You know she did," she chided. "I hope you slept."

He laughed heartily. "You know I did." He winked.

How she envied him, though she couldn't help sharing a laugh. It was nice, laughing with him. As if they were friends, partners.

If not lovers. If not man and wife in anything more than name only.

The ringing of the doorbell brought their laughter to a halt and wedged a block of ice into Cate's abdomen where her stomach had only just been.

"I have faith in you," Landon said, his fingers wrapping around hers for the briefest moment. Perhaps it should not have come as a surprise that his hand was as cold as hers.

Little did he know what it meant to hear those five simple words. To know someone had faith in her. All her life, she'd been treated like a baby. Spoiled, petted, and she had naturally enjoyed the treatment. Who wouldn't?

Yet that treatment was, in essence, a double-edged sword. For there was no separating the two—the petted, spoiled child, and the child who was unable to think, speak, or fend for herself. She could not be the adored youngest child of the family and hope to ever be treated as a woman.

Never had they told her they believed in her, because they didn't. She did not even think they understood what it would have meant to her had they given her just a bit of credit, a bit of respect.

Strange, but knowing he believed in her made her want them to believe in her, too. She liked the feeling of confidence it inspired, hearing someone placed their faith in her.

She knew very well as she lifted Violet from her crib that he was more than likely only telling her what he felt she needed to hear, to bolster her as they descended the stairs and opened the front door. Yet she still appreciated it, for he was kind and thoughtful even while under a terrible amount of pressure. He still took the time to think of her.

She waited at the foot of the stairs while Landon went to the door.

"Courage," she said with a smile in hopes of bolstering him as he had bolstered her.

He flashed a grateful grin before reaching for the doorknob and turning it.

It was now or never.

15

He told himself this was nothing more than a matter of jumping into a body of freezing water all at once, before common sense could stop him.

In such situations, common sense was a deterrent. It warned a person against leaping, against the cold their body was sure to suffer upon touching the water.

A man could spend his entire life dipping his toes into cold water, questioning himself, thinking he might be better off waiting for the water to warm up a bit.

It was far easier to get the deed over with straightaway, to jump in and allow the body to adjust as it would.

That was what he did when he opened the door to his home. He got it over with all at once.

"Welcome!" he nearly shouted, and he hoped they would interpret this as eagerness rather than terror. "Welcome to our home."

As ever, his parents spoke at once, their voices over-lapping.

His father, always the practical one, strode inside while leaving his baggage on the porch. He removed his top hat, loosening the woolen muffler around his neck.

"This is hardly the first time we have seen your home, son. Have you forgotten?" He looked and sounded the same as he had the last time Landon saw him. Energetic, boister-ous, in spite of the silver hair which threatened to overtake the black.

Meanwhile, his mother had truly heard what he said. "*Our* home?" She followed her husband, her step a bit less certain. She looked up at Landon, her blue eyes filled with questions.

It pained him to see a greater number of fine lines around the corners which wrinkled when she squinted through her round spectacles.

He nodded, grinning, lifting his arm to gesture toward the young woman and baby at the foot of the stairs.

Looking back at her, for just one moment he found himself believing that she was his wife, that this was all real. How proud he would be to call her his. She made a lovely image, the very picture of young motherhood.

"Mother, Father, I would like you to meet my wife, Cate. And your granddaughter, Violet."

His parents' reactions were predictable. Oliver remained in place, gaping at Cate and Violet. He was the type who took a moment to truly understand such occur-rences before reacting.

Hermione, on the other hand, did not wait to remove her coat before hurrying across the hall. "My granddaughter?" she breathed, holding her arms out for the baby. "She is my granddaughter?"

Cate handled this beautifully, handing the baby over for inspection with a shy smile and a hint of color in her cheeks. "Yes, she is. This is Violet. She is two months old."

Landon watched, his heart swelling, as his mother held the baby in the crook of her arm. The look of pure wonder on her face seemed to erase twenty years, turning her into a young woman simply overwhelmed with the joy of holding a beloved baby. "Goodness gracious! When were you going to tell us about this?"

"To say nothing of the fact that you now have a wife." Oliver still looked perplexed, though he clapped Landon on the back and laughed heartily. "You are certainly one for keeping secrets, are you not?"

Landon was careful to avoid Cate's gaze upon hearing this, knowing he would either laugh or do something to give them away if their eyes met. If they only knew the secrets that were being kept.

Hermione turned to him, looking as if she wanted to scold but was entirely unable to do so. "You were wed, and you did not tell us? You couldn't even so much as send a telegram?"

He had predicted this, and in his more rational moments could completely understand why this question would arise. After all, he had spoken not a word of either a wife or child.

"It happened rather suddenly. That is my marriage, if not the child," he chuckled, looking from one parent to the other. "We met while I was traveling, and the ceremony was not anything more than a visit to the Justice of the Peace. I wanted to surprise you. After all, I knew you would be visiting for the holidays, and with father so busy with his work I knew it would put a strain on both of you. You would want to come earlier. You would want to meet Cate and Violet, so I chose to hold my tongue and wait. I hope you are not too disappointed in me for having done so."

"Disappointed?" Hermione merely clicked her tongue while gazing down in adoration at her granddaughter. Landon sent up a silent prayer of thanks for the fact that she merely gazed back up at her grandmother without crying or carrying on. It was a beautiful moment, worth all of the deception and strain he had been under.

Oliver went to her, looking frankly amazed at this turn of events. "My, she reminds me a great deal of you when you were born."

He looked up at Cate then and laughed. "And you are our daughter-in-law!"

Hermione laughed, as well. "Heavens, I hope you do not think me rude for having ignored you. This is all such a surprise!"

"Cate, is it?" his father asked, taking Cate by the arms and kissing her cheek. "I hope you do not find me too forward, but this is a great pleasure. My wife and I have long hoped Landon would settle down and know the happiness of the family and home. And he did choose well."

Cate blushed prettily. "Thank you, sir. I believe I chose well, too." It was the perfect response, as both of his parents laughed merrily with her. He could not help but feel proud. She was doing beautifully.

"You may call me Hermione," his mother said. "This is such a wonderful surprise. I'm afraid I do not know what to do with myself. I'm so happy!"

"Why don't we all have seat in the parlor, and the two of you might remove your coats and be more comfortable." Landon brought their bags in from the porch, where they still sat for the lack of anyone remembering to bring them inside after finding a surprise in store for them, then joined them around the fire.

Hermione had yet to let go of Violet, and as such sat down in the chair still wearing her coat and hat.

"Father, allow me to pour you a drink. Is there anything either of you would like? I'm sure you're fatigued after your journey."

"Not at all, my boy!" Oliver's chest puffed out, the proud grandfather. "Why, it seems the trains go faster every day. I predict that before the end of the century, riding from one coast to the other will take no more than a few days."

"I wish that had been true while I was traveling." Landon poured them both a drink, one eye always on the women.

Hermione murmured one question after another in regard to the baby. Cate appeared to be handling it well.

The two of them shared a quiet laugh, making him wonder what joke they'd shared. He wished he could listen without making it look as though he was listening.

"How did the two of you meet?" Hermione asked, looking from one of them to the other.

Cate's eyes met his, and he spoke before she had the chance. He had not truly considered this. "We met at the theater, in fact."

He did a bit of rapid calculation in his head before continuing. "It was in Chicago, the first leg of my journey. By the time I left for St. Louis, we were married, and we had a bit of an unconventional honeymoon in St. Louis and then on to New York."

"I do adore New York," Cate murmured to Hermione, the two of them laughing as if they were already old friends.

"And by the time you returned, you had a child," Hermione marveled. "I don't know how you did it."

Cate shrugged. "To be honest, I was quite relieved to finally reach our home. It was nice to settle down. After all, what woman does not wish to set up housekeeping in a home of her own rather than in a hotel?" Yes, that was the perfect thing to say.

"Oh, heavens. I know all too well what that is like. My husband's work with the government has always kept him quite busy, and in the early days, I accompanied him from one place to the other. I'm fairly certain I have crossed Massachusetts enough times to know the terrain by heart."

"Now, Mother." Oliver smiled fondly at his wife. "Do

not forget that it was your presence at my side which helped me win the election."

"I find that quite admirable," Cate smiled. "You never know. Perhaps one day, you might decide to go into politics yourself. If such a time ever comes that women are allowed to do so. You will know everything there is to know before you even get started!"

Landon shot her a warning look before draining his glass. That had been a misstep.

Oliver sputtered. "Oh? Are you of such a mind that women ought to be allowed to vote? And to hold office?"

Landon spoke before she had the chance. "I'm sure Cate is only trying to be kind. She understands that you are of a rather conservative mindset and that any chance for women to play a role in the political landscape is nonexistent."

She blushed, lowering her eyes. "Of course." Yes, they would have to have a discussion about his father's political views. Was she not supposed to remain silent in hopes of avoiding such uncomfortable situations? How quickly she had forgotten her own assurances.

Quickly, she changed the subject. "It is nearly time for her evening feeding. Would you like to be the one to do so? We feed her by glass bottle," she informed Hermione. "There is a lovely rocking chair upstairs near the crib, and a warm fire. You might be able to make yourself more comfortable."

His mother nearly glowed with happiness. "I would love nothing more. Oh, if only I had known! I would have brought so many presents for the little one. She is so beautiful. Oh, how I have longed for a granddaughter to spoil terribly!"

The two of them laughed, their heads close to each other, and once again Landon was happier than he could ever remember being. This was going so well, minor setbacks aside, and she was so very happy. He resolved then and there that no matter how much Cate's theater cost, it would be well worth it. He would even be her most ardent admirer, never missing a performance.

He clasped his father's shoulder in a gesture of affection. "And as for you. I can show you to your room, and I will help you upstairs with the bags. Mrs. Davis has gone home for the evening, but she prepared a lovely supper for us which I'm sure Cate can manage to serve."

She did her best to conceal any surprise this announcement brought her. They truly had had such little time to discuss things.

"Naturally, and I'm sure you are hungry after being on the train all day," she added.

"First, I must see to my granddaughter's supper." Hermione stared down at Violet as she stood, cooing and babbling softly to the baby while she and Cate left the room and ascended the stairs.

He let out a long sigh, feeling the tension drain from his neck and shoulders. This was working. This was working beautifully. All would be well.

"I had considered the idea prior to our arrival, but now

it seems there is no choice." Oliver finished his drink, placing the glass on the serving tray and chuckling.

"What idea is that?"

"I thought it might do your mother world of good to extend the length of our stay. Now, I'm afraid I would not be able to drag her away if I tried. Perhaps we shall stay for a week. Or two. We might even remain through Christmas."

16

"He wants to stay longer. Perhaps through Christmas."

Cate turned to him, her mouth hanging open. It was bad enough she had to make sense of what Mrs. Davis had left them for supper and to serve it in a dignified manner, but this? "You know I can't stay that long."

Landon heaved an exasperated sigh. "Of course I know that. Which is why I'm telling you now. You simply have to find a way to extend your stay."

"But I can't!" she whispered, always careful to keep her voice low. Hermione was upstairs with the baby, while Oliver freshened up and rested. Even so, the walls were thin, and she would not wish to give them away so soon.

"You will simply have to work something out with Phoebe."

"Oh, yes. Phoebe. Because she seemed to be so

supportive of this scheme when we last saw her. I am sure she would go out of her way to help us now."

"We have no choice."

"Perhaps I can say I must visit my sister at the ranch? I can tell them she is expecting—that is not a lie—and that she is feeling poorly?" It was the best she could do on the spur of the moment.

Landon at least appeared to think this over. "I don't know. That might bring up too many painful memories for my mother."

She winced. "Fair enough, but I can say I need to go to the ranch. There is some trouble there that needs tending to."

"No! You can't say that! What am I thinking?" He ran his hands through his hair, pacing the length of the kitchen. "You're supposed to be from the east, remember? That is where we met. There would be no reason for you to have a sister on a ranch here."

Cate groaned, holding her face in her hand. "Of course. I ought to write these things down, so I can keep them straight. I am from Chicago, not Carson City. Can I at least pretend to be from Baltimore? That would not be a lie. I might have been traveling in Chicago, visiting family."

He nodded, distracted. "Yes, yes. That's fine. You might lend the story an air of legitimacy if you speak of places you know. I'm sorry, but there is simply no way for you to excuse your not being here."

"Yes, there is. And if your father has even a modicum of sensitivity and discretion, he will not ask for a specific reason as to why I must be away for a few days. I can always say I have a friend in need. For heaven's sake, your parents seem to be reasonable people. You behave as though they lack all understanding."

"So far, things have gone to their liking. Wait and see how my father reacts when something does not go the way he wishes. You saw the way his jaw dropped when you even suggested a woman's presence in politics."

Yes, that had been a misstep on her part. She had felt the change in the room almost instantly once the words had left her mouth. Just the memory made her uneasy.

"I simply do not understand why you would have to rearrange your entire life and any plans you had from now until Christmas simply because your father decided on a whim to stay longer than he had intended to. If I had planned to go visiting, why should I have to disappoint a friend who expects me?"

Landon gritted his teeth, glaring at her. "Do you forget why we're doing this? I don't mean for the sake of your theater. If you were my wife, and my parents decided to extend their visit, I would expect you to fall in line."

Her eyes widened, and she took a step back. "Oh. You would expect me to fall in line? Would you then expect me to wear a yoke around my neck, or perhaps a collar and lead? As if I were your dog?"

He rolled his eyes. "Must everything be so dramatic?"

"Pardon me, but I tend to be dramatic when a man speaks to me as if I were his slave."

"What is it, then? Cattle, a dog, or a slave?"

She glared at him, spitting her words out. "It depends upon how you choose to treat me, sir."

He waved his hands, shaking his head. "Enough of this. It is a moot point, since we are not really married. "

"Yes, we are." She raised her left hand as proof. "And we have a marriage license, which incidentally was granted us by the Justice of the Peace here in Carson City. Not in Chicago. That was a bad bit of explanation on your part."

"What was I supposed to say? That we waited until we arrived in Carson City to be married? That would hardly explain the presence of a two-month-old child in the house."

Yes, that made sense. "I suppose we could always pretend we lost the original marriage license in our travels," she mused, chewing on her lip. "For heaven sakes, we could have pretended that all along! We did not need to truly be married at all!"

He appeared truly stricken at this. "Pardon me if I did not think this through completely. In case you've forgotten, this is all rather spur of the moment. Some of it might have been worked out had my father not completely upended his schedule."

Yes, and she was beginning to tire of his father already. An old windbag, at least that was her first impression of him. Imagine, looking at her the way he had for only suggesting a woman one day take part in government. For heaven's sake.

"I must get supper on the table," she muttered, pushing her way past him a bit more forcefully than strictly necessary, but she was in a temper and more overwhelmed than she could ever remember feeling.

Could she possibly hope to extend her stay? It was bad enough Roan would have to lie to her sisters on her behalf. This would mean adding more lies on top of that, and her conscience already plagued her enough.

Hermione surprised them both by suddenly appearing in the doorway, then appeared to think better of it when she saw their expressions and the way they stood as if poised to fight.

"Is there anything I can do to help?" she asked, looking from one of them to the other.

Cate understood how it must look, as though she'd stepped into a domestic squabble. Well, they were fighting, but it was important for Hermione not to know this.

She forced a bright smile, shaking her head. "Not at all! You are a guest here. You are required to do nothing but relax and enjoy yourself and get to know your grand-daughter."

Her mother-in-law was not to be put off so easily. "Yes, but the little angel is asleep, and I thought it best to allow her to do so undisturbed. I did so wish to continue holding her, but that is how bad habits start. When a baby becomes accustomed to being held always, they tend to expect it and fuss terribly when they're put down."

Cate made a mental note of this. That might explain why Violet only seemed happy when she was being held. Perhaps Violet's own mother had spoiled her that way.

"Besides," Hermione added with a shy smile, "I've never

had a daughter, and have always longed for one. I would like to get to know you better."

What a choice of words. As if Cate needed reminding of the seriousness of the situation. Perhaps one of her lost babies had been a girl.

With this in mind, she handed Hermione an apron which hung on the hook behind the pantry door. "By all means, if you would not mind helping me dish out the delicious roast which Mrs. Davis so kindly prepared for us."

Landon appeared as if he wished to linger, likely out of concern for what Cate might say, but Hermione was having none of it. She placed her hands on his shoulders, turning him in place before pushing him out into the hall. "Now, now. This is my chance to get to know your wife better. You just go about your business and leave domestic matters to the women."

Landon looked absolutely terrified, but he did his mother asked. Cate wondered if he had lost faith in her, if he ever had any at all.

She resolved more firmly than ever to do well for his sake.

"I would love to hear all about when Landon was a little boy," she whispered with a wink. Anything to keep the conversation away from herself.

But Hermione was too quick for that. "It is you I want to know about. I would like to know the sort of girl my son chose. Which is not to say I disapprove of you," she was quick to add, "but I feel we will have so little time to know each other and do so wish to know you."

Naturally. "What is it you wish to know?" she asked, keeping her back turned while she pulled a pan of biscuits from the oven where they had been left to stay warm.

She was an actress. She could do this. She simply had to play the role of an adoring wife and happy, young mother. I could not be so difficult, could it?

"Where do you come from? Do you have family? What are they like?"

She supposed she could be mostly honest about this. It would be important to tell the truth whenever possible, to avoid keeping one lie after another straight. "I have four sisters, all of them older. My parents divorced when we were quite young, and we were raised by our mother. She came from a fine old family."

"Do they live in Chicago?"

"Actually, I was only visiting friends in Chicago. I did not make my home there. We lived in Baltimore."

"Baltimore! A lovely town."

"Have you been there?"

"Oh, yes. My husband's work takes him into Washington quite often, you see. Baltimore is not far from there."

"Of course not, how silly of me. I hadn't considered it." This was good. This would give them common ground on which they might meet.

"Your sisters live out there, then?"

"Yes, they do. My sister Holly is a schoolteacher. Molly works at the *Baltimore Sun*. Rachel works in a telegraph office, while Phoebe is a housekeeper. You see, while our mother's family was quite well-off, there is only so much left of our inheritance. We decided it was important to make our own way and save what was left."

This was good, as well. Hermione's eyes, so like Landon's, lit up. "Very wise of you. I understand what it means to consider one's future and practice discretion when it comes to the earning, saving, and spending of money. It does my heart good to know my son has found an intelligent wife and not a wasteful spendthrift."

Cate did what she could to keep from smiling in triumph. Wouldn't he be surprised when he learned of the success she was making of this. If anything, his presence only complicated matters. She did just fine on her own.

"You must tell me everything there is to know about my granddaughter," Hermione insisted as she lifted a glistening roast from the pan and set it on a delicately painted platter with gilt edges. Considering that she had not been there to choose the listed items herself, Cate could not help but be impressed with Landon's taste. He has done well on his own. He had merely needed guidance.

"She is a delight, isn't she?"

Hermione nodded, eager. "Though I am certain it cannot be easy for you, especially as so much of your early days with her were spent going from one place to the other."

"She is a well-tempered baby," Cate explained, wondering if she was saying the right things. "Besides, when they are so young, one place is just as good as another for them. At least, that is what I imagine."

"Yes, I can understand that. Is that why you decided

against nursing? I'm sure it would be terribly inconvenient, going from one place to the next while the baby needed to be fed."

Cate turned away, confused and terribly embarrassed. She had not expected such an intimate question, though she recalled some of the more delicate subjects her mother's friends had discussed while sitting around the whist table.

Hermione let out a groan of disappointment behind her. "Oh, my dear. Have I shocked you? Forgive me. I'm so accustomed to speaking frankly on these subjects with my married friends. You are not as accustomed to discussing these things as I am. Naturally, it is entirely none of my business."

Cate decided to leave it at that, as anything she hoped to say after that would be undoubtedly tongue-tied and awkward.

It seemed both marriage and motherhood were a minefield, with the promise of danger on all sides. She would do well to remember this.

"Do not wear yourself out. I will bring the food to the table. You might let Mr. Jenkins know supper is ready to be served," Cate suggested with a smile, lifting the serving platter.

"Please, dear. You might call him Oliver, if you feel comfortable doing so. Better yet, Father." Hermione was already halfway down the hall before Cate found the breath with which to speak.

Father? Oh, heavens.

Neither of them had considered what they would do once this visit was finished. Or how attached Mr. and Mrs. Jenkins might become to the daughter-in-law who would no longer be theirs.

What would happen when Landon had to admit they'd separated?

And what did it matter to her? They were strangers, and they would remain strangers. She would have what she wanted, what she'd always wanted, and this lovely woman with her careworn face and sweet, gentle voice would not have to suffer the shock of knowing her granddaughter was illegitimate.

She supposed that was as much as they could hope for, but it did little to assuage the guilt whose roots spread deeper with every lie she told.

17

"I must say, whatever you pay this Mrs. Davis is not nearly enough. She missed her calling when she did not become a professional chef de cuisine." Oliver sighed in approval, one hand over his stomach as he leaned back in his chair. He had certainly out-eaten all of them, going back for third helpings long after the others were finished.

"I suspect much of this has to do with the lack of proper dining as of late," Hermione explained. "One does tire of eating in restaurants and hotels after a while. A home-cooked meal means the world when it has been so long since we've enjoyed one."

As far as Landon was concerned, what his mother described was the ideal life. Having his every need seen to. He would certainly not complain if called upon to live the rest of his life that way.

Then again, looking around the table, it seemed there

might be something to be said for what he had at present. Domesticity, pride in one's home and one's family.

Now, he only needed an actual family. More than just his parents. A wife. A fine wife who would do him proud.

He suspected Cate might be a wife a man could be proud of, but that would never do. She was too flighty, too strange in her ways. Far too stubborn and hardheaded.

And, on top of everything else, she wanted to be an actress. Actresses were hardly the type to make decent wives.

He could not help but catch her eye from time to time and was regretful he'd been so sharp with her in the kitchen. She was only doing her best, just as he was, and he had an advantage over her, in that he knew his parents. She did not and had not been given proper time to acquaint herself with their ways.

He had promised her the time and had failed to deliver it. Anything that went wrong past this point was entirely his doing. He would do well to remember that.

"Landon tells me you are considering extending the length of your stay," she murmured, wiping the corners of her mouth with her napkin.

Well, he could not take the blame for this. She should have known how to hold her tongue, as she had promised him she would do. He'd forgotten to make mention of this when they were alone in the kitchen.

His father glanced across the table at his mother, a flash of regret crossing his face. "I had considered it, as we are both so delighted to have been presented with both you and our granddaughter. I had not yet discussed it with my wife, however."

Cate touched her hands to her cheeks, aghast. "I'm so sorry. I spoke out of turn. It is simply that I was so pleased to hear the news."

Landon groaned inwardly. She certainly could overdo it when she set her mind to it.

Hermione's mouth fell open. "Nothing would give me more pleasure. The more time I get to spend with the baby, the better. I already miss her. Isn't that strange? I miss her, yet she sleeps just above our heads."

Landon chuckled, glancing Cate's way. "Do not say that so loudly. She might hear you and decide to cry."

Hermione beamed, radiant. "I would not mind in the least. I would adore her no matter what she did."

"I understand what you mean. Not until a woman has a child of her own can she understand how it is possible to love that child no matter what they do. I suppose I could forgive Violet anything." Cate made a point of meeting Landon's eyes as she raised a glass of port.

Yes, she could definitely drive a point home when she set her mind to it.

"I have felt that way about Landon here his entire life," Hermione admitted, reaching across the table for his hand.

Hers was a familiar hand, the feeling of it around his one of the first memories he could recall of his childhood. How she had guided him, molded him, taught him to be the man he was.

A forgiving mother. A loving, sweet mother.

But he could not bring himself to believe she would forgive him if she knew the truth of Violet's parentage. That, he could not ask her to forgive. He would not even know the words to use should he begin asking for her forgiveness.

Rather than allow Cate to run away with the conversation, he turned to his father. "Tell me, how are things in Washington?"

"Oh, please. Forgive me, but are we to speak of politics tonight? I have not seen you in so long, and I do wish to know more about your wife." Hermione squeezed his hand while looking to Cate.

Any other woman would have paled beneath her probing gaze. Cate, on the other hand, seemed to thrive under it. "We have plenty of time in which to get to know each other," she assured her. "There is a great deal I'd like to know about you, as well. And about your son. He is not as forthcoming with information about himself as he might be."

Oliver chortled. "Keeping secrets from your wife, eh, son?"

"Hardly," he replied, eyeing his wife with suspicion. "Just what is it you wish to know?"

"I would love to hear about you as a boy. What sort of child were you? Did you ever give your parents any trouble? Did you get up to mischief when you shouldn't have?"

His mother threw back her head, laughing gaily. Once again, he was struck by the way she seemed to grow younger. It had not occurred to him until then just how rare it was to see her enjoy herself, to truly let loose and feel free to laugh and tease.

"I must say, looking back, he could have been much worse. Some of his boyhood chums got into terrible scrapes when they were growing up." She looked to Oliver, her eyes twinkling. "Do you recall the time they ran pigs through the center of town?"

"How could I forget?" Oliver laughed.

Cate giggled helplessly. "He did not!"

Landon cleared his throat. "For the record, since no one here seems to care much about the facts of the story, I will tell you that it was an accident. We did not mean to open the gate to the pigpen. What the rest of the town thought of as us running the pigs through town was really nothing more than our attempts to corral the pigs and get them home."

It was clear no one at the table believed this story, as their laughter grew louder than ever. He decided to accept this and simply be glad for it, since this was going better than he ever could have imagined.

He owed it all to her. She understood instinctively that his parents would wish to share stories of their only child, and they sat back and listened as both of his parents regaled them with tales even he had forgotten over the years.

Cate's eyes shone as she looked from one of them to the other, following along as they picked up the threads of one memory after another, weaving them together until they created a tapestry which represented his life up to that point.

Once, she looked at him, and all artifice fell away. He saw, not his pretend wife, but the young woman he had found at the bank who'd had impressed him with her poise and bravery. They were still in this together, the two of them, partners.

He would rather have no one else as a partner in this.

"I have an idea," he suggested when they rose from the table. "Perhaps you could regale us with a dramatic recitation, dear heart."

Her eyes went perfectly round, her face flushing.

His father turned to her. "Oh? Do you know any pieces you could share?"

"Yes, please, do! I would so enjoy it." Hermione clasped her hands over her breast.

"I... ought to see to the dishes," she murmured, looking confused and very definitely unwilling to perform. "Truly, they should not be left for Mrs. Davis. Perhaps tomorrow evening, I will prepare something for you then."

"Are you certain, dearest?" Landon asked, giving her the sweetest, most sickening smile he could manage. Let her see what it felt like to be the center of attention when she wished for nothing less.

The look she gave him might have melted solid rock. "Yes, darling. Though if you would be willing to clean up, I would be only too pleased to entertain your parents."

He had no choice but to concede defeat with a gentle

tip of his head, laughing to himself all the while. She was quite an opponent.

"Come, Father. I know you enjoy a brandy after supper, just as I do," he offered, leading Oliver to the study while his mother followed Cate, picking up dishes from the table and carrying them to the kitchen.

He could almost allow himself to believe for a moment that this was real.

Oliver took a seat and accepted the brandy Landon offered. "I must say, son, that you chose very well. I admit, I was astounded when we arrived. She is quite young, though your mother was young when we married. I believe she will make an excellent wife for a man such as yourself. One who is going places in the world."

Hearing it set Landon's teeth on edge. They would be disappointed when this sham of a marriage fell apart, wouldn't they? He supposed he would deal with the aftermath when the time came. No sense worrying about it when there was still so much convincing to do.

"I'm sure you can see how happy this makes your mother," he added, swirling the liquid in the glass. "Truly, you could not have presented her with anything better during this visit. It thrills her to no end. I would not be surprised if she insisted on purchasing a home here, just so she can be nearer her granddaughter."

Landon found it difficult to swallow his drink now that there was a lump blocking his throat. "Perhaps I could make a point of visiting more often. That might make it easier on you."

"Or you might move east," Oliver suggested, almost leaping at the opportunity to present his idea. Landon wondered if he'd been waiting for just this opportunity all along.

"Why would I do that when I have a wonderful life here? And this house which you insisted on having built in my honor?" he laughed in an attempt to lighten the dread settling into his bones.

"There are many opportunities for a man such as yourself in Washington," his father argued. "Why, you've proven yourself indispensable here, and that reputation is sure to follow wherever you go. You would no longer be in the middle of nowhere. I'm certain your wife and daughter would be happier, with better access to... well, everything."

Landon finished his drink. "There is more than enough time to discuss all of this," he decided, putting the conversation to rest for the time being. He told himself he should have known his father would not be satisfied with the life he'd built in Carson City.

Even an excellent—if fake—wife would not be enough.

18

———

"Shh, sweet one. That's a good girl." Cate walked Violet up and down the length of the room as she had back at the ranch.

What she would not give for a good night's sleep.

While the baby did not wail as she was wont to do, she was fussy and whimpering and generally unhappy as Cate rubbed the sleep from her eyes before turning to walk another length with the baby on her shoulder. "Why can't you be a good girl like you were for your grandmother?" she hissed.

Perhaps there was something to be said for experience. When Hermione had fed her, she'd expelled the air from her belly and gone straight to sleep. She hadn't even spit up, which seemed a small miracle.

Cate had half a mind to wake Hermione now, since she was so fixed on doting on the baby.

A faint tap at the door separating her room from Landon's made her jump in surprise.

"Yes?" she whispered, closing her wrapper a bit tighter than before. It hadn't occurred to her that he might visit during the night, and she was glad she'd left her stays on for lack of anyone to lace her into the in the morning.

One of the many reasons she missed her sisters.

Landon stuck his head into the room, and she noted his handsome silk dressing gown which he'd belted over his nightshirt. While hardly an inch of him was exposed to her, she felt somehow as if she was seeing what she ought not see.

Yet he was her husband, legally and truly.

This didn't stop her from averting her eyes when he first entered.

"How is she?" he asked, his voice soft and low.

"Fussing terribly. I must admit, I'm tired."

"I know all too well what you mean. At least I slept last night. Here, allow me." He held his arms out for her. "I'll walk her for a while, so you can rest."

"Are you sure?"

"Cate. She is my daughter, after all. My responsibility. You've already done so much." His smile was so lovely. At least, it struck her as such at that moment. Perhaps it was fatigue or gratitude or both. She gave him the baby and sank into one of the two chairs near the window.

He made a handsome sight, patting Violet's back as he walked her the way Cate had just done. She noticed after a few minutes that he was humming as well, a tuneless sort of song which was pleasant just the same.

Violet certainly seemed to enjoy it, quieting soon after he'd started.

"You are a good father," Cate whispered, resting her head against the back of the chair.

"I certainly don't feel like one," he whispered in reply. "I feel like a terrible father, one who cheats his daughter out of what she deserves. Now I'm cheating my parents, too."

"It isn't your fault."

"It is."

"You didn't make that girl leave. You couldn't have known when you were away. You are being far too hard on yourself."

"That's very easy for you to say. I know you are only trying to spare my feelings."

She rolled her eyes and said no more, deciding against continuing the argument in favor of enjoying peace and quiet. It was so nice, with a fire flickering gently in the grate, causing shadows to dance on the opposite wall...

A moment later, Landon shook her shoulder. "Cate. Cate, wake up."

She blinked hard, noting the crick in her neck almost instantly. "What happened?" She looked up at him, his face very near hers. "Where are... what...?"

Why was he laughing at her? "You fell asleep. The baby is sleeping in her crib. I thought you ought to lie in bed rather than spend the night sitting up in the chair. I turned down the blanket for you."

How kind of him. "You are so—" She stopped herself in time. She was about to call him sweet, or perhaps handsome. Was she not? She hadn't fully woken up yet.

"Think nothing of it," he whispered as he helped her to her feet. "Come, now. We'll have a long day ahead of us."

"You know, I can find a way to stay. Here, I mean, without going home before your parents leave." She sat on the bed, the horsehair mattress soft yet firm enough that she did not sink straight into it. To her surprise, he bent to remove her slippers, then lifted her legs and swung them onto the bed as if he ever had right to do so.

If she had not been half-dead with exhaustion, she might have taken offense.

"That's funny." He chuckled under his breath, pulling the blankets over her. "I was just about to tell you not to worry. You are right, of course. There is no reason in the world why you would not go visiting a friend in need, even if your husband's parents were here for a visit. Leave it to me."

She smiled up at him, keenly aware of the intimacy of this moment and suddenly wishing it would go on forever. He stood over her while she burrowed beneath the blanket, her head resting on a pillow thick with goose feathers. Half of his face was cast in shadow, the rest barely revealed by the dying fire's light.

If this were one of the novels she loved so well, and if he were the sort of man who behaved in such a way, he might ravish her. It was his right as her husband, was it not? He could easily behave like a beast and use their marriage license to explain away his behavior.

To her surprise and dismay, her heart raced at the thought, and not out of horror or panic, but something else. Something she'd never felt before.

She, who believed herself so attuned to the wide range of human emotion, had never felt this before.

"Sweet dreams, Cate." He bent down, and for a moment she thought he was going to do what she'd vaguely imagined. That he had darker intentions in mind.

The breath caught in her throat. Her mouth went dry.

When his lips brushed her forehead, his stubble tickling her skin, she was both relieved and slightly disappointed.

He tiptoed from the room, closing the door with nothing more than a whisper.

Leaving her thoroughly perplexed and not at all certain she was the young lady her mother had raised.

"It is a beautiful day!" Hermione crowed upon entering the morning room. "Why, I nearly threw open the windows to let some of this unusually warm air into the house."

Indeed, it felt more like spring than mid-December outside. That, plus a healthy amount of sleep, left Cate feeling bright and cheerful that morning.

She tried to tell herself those few sweet moments with Landon had nothing to do with her disposition.

Cate held Violet out to her grandmother, the baby cooing happily when she rested in Hermione's arms. "Her little neck is so strong! Look at her holding her head up with so much confidence. Yes, she is a fine, strong girl." Hermione covered her cheeks with kisses and stroked the silky, blonde hair which covered her head.

Suddenly, she frowned. "Is blond hair a trait in your family?" she asked.

Would there be no end to these sudden surprises? "Blond hair?" Cate stalled.

"It's only that Oliver and Landon are black of hair, and mine is brown like yours. It strikes me as strange..."

"Oh, my hair was golden as a child. All of our hair was," she lied. "It darkened over time. My mother was fair-haired."

"Was she? How marvelous. Perhaps our Violet will remain fair. What do you think, sweetheart?" she asked, bouncing her gently.

Cate let out the breath she was holding, glad to have avoided another possible trap.

Until...

"We ought to take the baby for a stroll! It would do her good to be out in this wonderful fresh air. I don't think I've ever smelled air so fresh."

Cate gulped. A stroll? Through town? "Are you certain it would be good for her? After all, it could turn cold at any moment..." Where in the world was Landon when she needed him?

"She has a perambulator, does she not?"

"Yes, she does," she had to admit. It was one of the items Phoebe had suggested they add to the list.

"With a few extra blankets, she ought to be right as rain. What do you think, dear?" Hermione held her up, lifting her high into the air until she squealed and giggled.

She was a darling, and Cate fell more deeply in love with her all the time. What would she do once there was no reason for them to be together any longer?

She supposed if she wore a muffler, warmer weather or not, she might hide the lower part of her face. That could help. They need not walk the length of Carson Street more than once, and on a day such as this, there would be plenty of people out and about. They might blend in more easily that way.

So long as they avoided lingering near the jailhouse...

It was clear Hermione would not be refused, so Cate dragged her feet up the stairs and set about dressing herself for a morning stroll.

She heard Landon preparing himself for his day in the next room and knocked on the connecting door.

He opened it, his face half-covered in shaving lotion, still in his nightshirt. "What is it?" he asked when he noted the horror on her face.

Whether she was horrified by his mother or by the ease with which he revealed his private life to her, she could not say. Perhaps he was better accustomed to being free and easy with young ladies.

Perhaps that was what had gotten him into this mess, to begin with.

"She wants to take the baby for a walk throughout the town!" she hissed. "What am I to do? You know I can't dissuade her when she gets a notion in her head."

He looked stricken. "You might walk me to my office, and then come home. Tell her your head aches or something of the sort. She will believe there is plenty of time in which to take a stroll, and we can hope for frigid weather after today."

Yes, that would have to do. Except…

"Where is your office?" she asked. "You never told me."

He gaped at her, open-mouthed, before chuckling with a rueful expression. "I suppose it's just as well. It isn't as if my father would expect you to have any understanding of what I do, so he would never bring it up to you."

She bristled at this, biting her tongue to hold back a sharp retort. "Well? Where is it?"

"At the bank. I am vice-president."

Her eyes went perfectly round before she backed away, now trembling all over. "No."

He came to her, puzzlement written all over his half-masked face. The shaving lotion had now dried, and cracks had begun to form, giving him the look of a broken piece of pottery. "What is it?"

"You work for the bank. Now I understand everything. How could you?" she hissed. "You wanted to keep me here. You want me to lose the ranch, for my sisters to lose the ranch. It would go to the bank, and that's what the bank wants. How could I have been so blind?"

"Wait, wait!" He went to the door leading to the hall,

looking out as if to be certain they were alone before closing it again and turning to her. "Keep your voice down, please. I don't know where you got this idea from. It must be the strangest of all you've shared with me until now."

"I would thank you to keep your opinions to yourself, you treacherous thing."

He rolled his eyes. "Cate, this is not one of your plays. I am not some dastardly villain. In fact, none of us are. I do not know where you got that idea from. This has nothing to do with your ranch, and no one is trying to take it from you."

"Then why did you never mention before you were the vice-president of the bank?"

"How did you think I found you? Why did you think I was at the bank that day?"

"People go to the bank all the time! I assumed you were there doing some other sort of business!"

He shrugged, sighing heavily. "I suppose we both assumed a bit too much. Once again, we had no time to straighten these things out. I did not deliberately keep it from you. We simply never discussed it. My position at the bank has nothing to do with your ranch, and I frankly would rather see your sisters maintain ownership."

She eyed him with deep suspicion. "You would?"

"Yes. I have nothing to do with that. This is all I care about right now; my family, my parents, my child. I would never be part of some scheme to keep you away from what is rightfully yours. I mean this as kindly as I can manage; you must learn the difference between what happens in real life between two people and what happens in a play or a novel. You allow your imagination to run away with you and look how worked up you have allowed yourself to become over nothing at all."

She hated to admit that he was right about this, for she had indeed worked herself up into quite a state. She went to the washbasin on the stand and splashed her face with cold water in hopes of bringing her color back to a more normal hue. "Forgive me. I did get away from myself, and that was unfair to you."

"All is forgiven. Now, hurry. Mother will wonder what is taking you so long to appear."

To her horror, his words brought to mind a number of images which might explain her lingering upstairs with her husband while Hermione tended the baby downstairs. Her cheeks blazed once again, and she splashed them after he had left the room to return to his grooming.

She had flown off the handle for no reason. Landon had not given her any reason to doubt him up to this point, had he? He did not seem the type to use another in so callous a manner.

And the odds of seeing Rance or Mason or even Rachel as she drove to the ranch were slim, were they not? Nearly non-existent, really. This was nothing more than a tempest in a teapot.

Perhaps Landon and the girls were all correct, and she did need to bring her imagination to heel. It did tend to run away with her at the most inopportune times.

Within twenty minutes, with Landon enjoying a quick

breakfast while standing at the table in the morning room, the four of them were off. "Father says he intends to spend the morning catching up on correspondence," Landon explained as they descended the front stairs, all of them breathing deep of the fresh, unseasonably warm air.

Hermione merely shook her head, clicking her tongue disapprovingly. "I had so hoped he would get a bit of rest on this trip. It seems he never stops working." She turned to Cate then, casting a knowing look her way. "I suppose you had best become accustomed to that, as well."

Cate frowned. "What do you mean?"

"It's merely that the men of this family tend to place work very highly on the list of things they believe are important."

Landon wound his arm around his mother's with a fond smile. "Father's work is very important. You of all people should know that."

"Yes, but I fear it took him away from us too frequently. I do not profess to know all there is to know about what he does, but there were many times..." She did not continue, her voice catching at the end.

Though she knew she ought not to allow her imagination to take flight, Cate could only imagine how Hermione had needed Oliver in the days after the loss of their children. Perhaps that was what she referred to. Perhaps he'd not been as available to her as she would have liked. Perhaps she had no one to turn to.

Cate decided then and there that if she ever were to marry, she would want a partner. Someone who would not only support her in her times of need, but who would allow her to support him and then give credit where it was due.

While Oliver did not seem an entirely bad sort, and she could admit her original opinion of him might have been made in haste, she still had the feeling he was the type too blind to see just how much of his current success was possible because of his devoted wife.

She could not think about that any longer, for they were nearly at Carson Street. Her hands tightened around the perambulator's handlebar as she pushed it before her. At least Violet seemed to be enjoying herself, looking around in wonder at everything they passed.

"What an impressive building!" Hermione marveled as they neared the bank. "To think, my son is vice-president of this bank. We are so proud of you."

Though Landon tried to hide it, his pleasure was evident. It meant a great deal to him, knowing he could impress his mother and make her proud. Cate tried to imagine what it would be like to hold her parents' entire lifetime's worth of hopes and dreams on her shoulders.

"Have a nice day," Cate said as they came to a stop. It was more important than ever to avoid notice, and she could not help but cast one worried look after another in the direction of the jailhouse. All she needed was for Rance or Mason to step out and find her there, pretending to be the happy wife and mother she was not.

"Well?" Hermione asked, looking from her son to her daughter-in-law.

"Well...?" Landon looked her way, confused, and she shrugged.

Hermione chuckled. "You might give your wife a brief kiss on the cheek. After all, you will not see her until this evening. I would not mind."

Now, this was too much.

Cate blushed uncontrollably as she turned to her husband. He looked greatly uncomfortable, as well, but appeared willing to appease his mother if nothing else.

He leaned down, barely brushing his lips against her cheek.

Meanwhile, her eyes darted back and forth, as she hoped and prayed no one would see this. Were all mothers-in-law as pestering as Hermione? Perhaps next she would ask when to expect her second grandchild.

"Good luck," he whispered with a knowing look.

If she did not know better, she would swear he was fleeing the scene in hopes of avoiding further embarrassment.

All right for him, then. He could run into the bank and leave her alone to manage his mother and child all on her own. She hoped he was prepared to pay quite a lavish sum for the creation of her theater, for she deserved it after this.

He looked up, over her shoulder, and his eyes widened as if in alarm.

"What is it?" she whispered while Hermione fussed over the baby. "What's wrong?"

She turned as well, following the direction of his gaze, but all she saw were people walking in both directions and a number of buggies and wagons rolling down the center of the street.

"Nothing," he muttered, his voice as distant as his gaze, before turning and leaving. She watched him disappear behind the heavy doors with a sinking heart. How could she manage this alone?

She turned to Hermione, intending to feign a headache or some other malady which would give her an excuse to go home just as she and Landon had planned, when the sight of a familiar buggy caught her eye as it rolled down the street.

She turned her face away, her heart racing madly, her stomach suddenly threatening to surrender its contents. It was Rachel; it had to be. Or Phoebe. Or both of them, on their way home. They had seen her. There was no getting her imagination to settle down now.

"Did Landon seem out of sorts to you?" Hermione asked when they were alone, unaware of Cate's distress.

"I suspect he has been under a great deal of strain as of late," she offered by way of explanation, scrambling madly for something suitable to say. "It is quite a change for him. For both of us," she added. "The marriage, the baby. He is still settling into his new routine."

"Of course, of course. My mother's intuition is getting ahead of me, I suppose." If she noticed Cate's distress, she spoke nothing of it.

"I do not feel well," she murmured, pressing her hand to her forehead. It was not entirely untrue, as the certainty that she just been spotted by her sisters sent wave after wave of nausea rolling over her. "Do you think we could take this walk another time? I hope the good weather holds out and gives us the ability to do so."

"Of course! You must rest once we return to the house. I will take care of everything." If anything, Hermione looked pleased as punch at the prospect of caring for her granddaughter.

Yes, she needed to rest. She had to close her eyes and get her thoughts in order, or she might do something drastic—such as telling the truth and having the whole thing over with.

As much as she wanted her theater, she began to question whether it was worth the effort and the strain she had already gone through.

19

It couldn't have been her. It simply couldn't have
been.

Cate hadn't noticed, and she wouldn't, since she
did not know what Ida looked like. She had not noticed the
golden-haired woman standing across the street, staring at
them in surprise and recognition and perhaps more than a
bit of dismay.

No, she'd been far too enveloped in her own concerns.
That was as he supposed it should be.

Just as it was up to him to handle Ida if she had, indeed,
returned to town.

Funny thing, that. He'd wanted nothing more for than
for her to return for the first week in which she had been
gone. Now, he wanted nothing more than for her to stay
away, at least until this whole matter was settled and his
parents were none the wiser.

Once again, he spent the morning utterly wrapped up

in his personal concerns rather than those of the bank. Letters, messages, and reports sat untouched on his desk while he stared out the window and asked himself if he had only been seeing things. While he never would have thought himself the type before this, the strain on his nerves might just have been enough to cause his over-wrought mind to conjure images which were not real.

It was roughly noon when one of the bank's errand boys approached his office door. "Sir, there is a lady to see you." He both looked and sounded utterly scandalized at the thought of a woman being present in the bank.

His heart sank, though he had expected all along. He had only been waiting for Ida to decide it was time to reveal herself once again.

He supposed he ought to consider himself lucky that she had chosen the bank, rather than appearing at his doorstep. There was no telling what might have happened had she chosen that route.

"You may show her in," he replied with an air of resignation. What was the use in hiding? It was always better to get such things over with as quickly as possible.

His surprise, when the woman in question was not the golden-haired, pink-cheeked Ida he recalled, but rather a dark-haired young woman whose eyes blazed in fury, could not have been greater. He might have asked who she was, might even have demanded, if the resemblance was not so clear. This was another one of Cate's sisters.

And, judging from the way she clearly attempted to

conceal her swelling belly, he judged her to be Molly. Molly was the one Cate was always the most worried about.

And once she opened her mouth to speak, he could understand why. "Perhaps you could help me with something," she said without waiting for a proper introduction. "You see, my sister has been away from home for days, after arriving at our home with a very young child in her care. She then disappeared without warning, with our brother-in-law providing at best half-hearted excuses as to why she had suddenly gone. Now, I hear she was seen with you this morning. Standing in front of the bank, baby in a perambulator, while you kissed her on the cheek. Who in the world are you, really, and what business have you with my sister?"

He hardly knew what part of her tirade to address first. He stood, walking around the desk that he might pull out a chair. "Please, have a seat. Is there anything I can get for you?"

She remained in place, hands folded before her. "You can get me the truth," she insisted. A stubborn one. He saw where Cate got it from.

"It is a rather long story, and I would feel better if you took a seat before I began it. Please, I can explain everything."

To say she was suspicious would be a great understatement, yet she took the chair he offered and sat ramrod straight, her eyes never leaving his for a moment. This was a woman who could only be described as formidable, and he understood now why Cate had been concerned about her most of all.

He sat across from her, more nervous than he would have liked to admit. "How did you know who I was? I might have been any man about to head into the bank."

"It seems another of my sisters was aware of this arrangement you have with Cate, and she mentioned your name."

"Then you knew. You came here, questioning me, when you knew all along. I would imagine Phoebe told you all of it."

She stiffened. "You might refer to her as Mrs. Connelly," she murmured.

He winced at his clumsiness. "Pardon me, of course. It is only that Cate so often speaks of all of you, I have come to think of you by your first names."

Molly sniffed, unimpressed. "She speaks of us? I must admit, that comes as a surprise. It is rare that Cate thinks of anyone but herself."

"With respect, madam, I do not believe you give her the credit she is due."

"With respect, sir, you don't know what you're talking about. I have known my sister her entire life, and this situation, while appalling, is nothing I would ever put past her."

He sized her up, using the same instincts which had always served him well in business. While on the surface she was hard, even cold, he sensed a deep well of concern. Love, though he suspected she would have been loath to admit it to a stranger.

He called to mind what Cate had told him about her family up to this point. The passing of both parents, the way her sisters banded together to support themselves upon the loss of their mother. Molly was the oldest and would, therefore, have taken on the role of a mother figure to the rest.

He suspected that were Cate one of his sisters and were he responsible for her well-being, he would be driven to distraction as well.

With this in mind, he took another tack. "The responsibility falls entirely on me. Your sister came to the bank to seek funds for a theater she wished to open."

Molly rolled her eyes. "Yes, I am aware of this."

He did wish she would hold her tongue. It must have been a family trait, the inability to allow a man to finish a story. "As I was saying, I happened to be present, and I felt sorry for her. She was so earnest and poised in spite of the derision she faced from the bank's president. Perhaps if she had come to me first instead of attracting his notice, I could have handled her more gently. He laughed at her, and she left. I followed her out, both wanting to comfort her and wanting to know just how serious she was about obtaining this funding. You see, I have more than enough at my disposal, and I was desperately in need of help."

"It is that help, as you call it, that I wish to discuss. Is it true that you married her?"

There was no avoiding the truth. "Yes. We were married by the Justice of the Peace, and as I promised, the marriage will be annulled just as soon as possible. I wanted our union to be legitimate."

"This is all in service of hiding the fact that your

daughter was born..." She shifted in her chair, suddenly uncomfortable. She'd been raised as a lady, after all, and as such would be uncomfortable speaking of such matters.

He, on the other hand, was no lady. He was hardly even a gentleman, considering all he had already done. "Yes, my daughter's mother bore her while I was traveling for business. She left her with me, then ran away. As I told Cate, I would have gladly made things right by marrying the girl, but she gave me no choice. She fled before we could make plans. That is the truth." Even so, he grimaced when he remembered the woman who had looked so much like Ida watching him from across the street that morning.

Molly's eyes were just a sharp as her sister's. "What are you not telling me? Come, now. I believe a brother and sister-in-law we should have no secrets."

Was it his imagination, or was there a note of enjoyment in her voice? As if she was having fun with this against her better judgment?

"You see, I did not speak to Cate of this, but I saw a woman who looked very much like Violet's mother just before entering the bank this morning. She appeared to be watching me, my mother and Cate on the sidewalk. Perhaps this is nothing more than an overreaction on my part. After all, Ida's appearance would ruin everything. My parents already adore your sister, just as they love Violet, and while it is one thing to break their hearts when they believe we have divorced, it would be entirely another to admit this was a lie along."

Molly frowned, her brows knitting together just as

Cate's did when she was disturbed. "What is her name? The girl, I mean."

"Ida Thomas. She lived on a farm outside of town, and I can only imagine she went back there if she did in fact return. Her family was quite poor, I know that much, though she possessed a great deal of intelligence and poise and seemed to wish to rise above her station. At least, that was what I told myself about her. Why I'd share any of this with you now is a mystery, but I suppose there is something to be said for having someone to confide in. As I said, I did not wish to upset your sister with this. She is already strained enough."

"This has been difficult for her?"

"For both of us. She doesn't wish to lie any more than I do. But you see, my mother has already experienced such disappointment is life. Her health has not been good in the last several years, and I did not wish to make things worse for her."

Molly raised an eyebrow. "Nor for your father, the powerful senator. You did not wish to cause a scandal for him."

He shrugged. "What can I say? Do not speak of it as if I'm in the wrong for wishing to spare them the pain."

"No, you're not in the wrong. I only wish you had not chosen my sister for this. You took advantage of her, and I do not find that easy to forgive. Nor will any of the rest of our sisters, nor our brothers-in-law."

He grimaced at the memory of the man who'd stormed into his house. "I have already met one of them, and I have no doubt he would take pleasure in pummeling me, if given the chance."

"Frankly, if Cate had had sense in her head, she would have refused you flat-out."

This, he could not stand. "Once again, I must contradict you. I believe you do her a disservice by underestimating her. She is quite keenly intelligent, eager to be of help. She has done beautifully with my daughter. In that respect, I know I could not have found a more suitable partner in this scheme. I trust her with Violet, which I cannot say about just anyone. She has gone out her way to please my parents, and to make this a success. Perhaps if you had not dismissed her out of hand so many times, she would not have seen fit to venture into a bank where she must have known she would not be wanted or respected. Perhaps she spent so much of her life being disrespected that she supposed this would be just one more instance for her to suffer. I could not say. But you were all too hard on her, and it does not surprise me in the least that she would resort to extreme measures when granted so little understanding by the people who are supposed to understand her best."

He shouldn't have said it. It was rude, disrespectful, but he could not help himself. He'd had just about enough of listening to his wife being underestimated. And someone had to defend her.

Molly was quiet for a long moment, her eyes moving back and forth over his face. When she spoke, he was surprised to find her tone softer than it had been before. After all, he had expected her to shoot up from her chair and deliver a brutal tongue-lashing after he'd spoken so freely.

"It appears as though I owe you an apology. While I still feel you have been foolish involving her in this, you appear to understand her. Perhaps even better than I do. It is not easy for the eldest sister to think of the youngest as anything more than a child. You have helped me understand how wrong I might have been. Though I cannot take responsibility for what she has done, for that was entirely her choice. I did not drive her to anything."

He had participated in enough negotiations to know when it was time to compromise. "That is fair."

"Perhaps I misjudged you both. It is a terrible situation you found yourself in. Both you and the young woman in question. If you wish, I might be of service."

Now, this was a surprise. "And just how would you do that?"

"What you have said about your... friend, Ida, got me thinking. I believe there is someone we can call into the service to help us determine whether she has truly returned to Carson City, and what she might have returned for."

He could hardly believe his ears. "Are you suggesting working with us on this?"

"So long as you promise not to tell Cate that I'm aware of what is going on. I don't want her to believe I approve of any of this. And I don't," she was quick to add. "But I do wish to make this easier on both of you if I can. The sooner this is finished, the better for all of us."

"I heartily agree." He half-stood, extending one arm across the desk in hopes of shaking her hand. She was a woman of good sense, and he respected that. He also respected the way she so fiercely protected her sister, even if she did not agree with her methods.

After the briefest hesitation, she shook his hand with a firm grip. It seemed the person Cate most worried about learning of their plan was to be their staunchest ally.

Perhaps they could make a success of this, after all.

20

———

"Mrs. Davis will be staying with us tonight, which means you will have the chance to enjoy our company after supper."

Cate cast a worried look Landon's way. "Why does that not make me feel better?"

He fastened her mother's string of pearls around her neck, his hands lingering perhaps a bit longer than necessary on her shoulders. "I thought you would be pleased. It will mean less work for you."

He was trying so hard to be of help. It warmed her heart, just as the touch of his hands on her shoulders did.

Of course, this also worried her greatly. It would not do for them to form an attachment, though she suspected that she had already done so, which was the one thing she should have guarded herself against.

How could she help herself? Looking at his reflection

above her own, his encouraging smile, knowing the faith he had in her. No one had ever had faith in her before.

No one had ever expected anything of her before.

How was she supposed to avoid falling in love with a handsome, kind, gentle man who believed in her?

Violet fussed in her crib, sending him across the room to check what was the matter. He was an attentive father when given the opportunity to be one. In other words, when he was not running about in a panic, doing everything in his power to solve little emergencies as they popped up here and there.

He bent over his daughter, whispering to her, and Cate wondered what the men at the bank would think if they knew how sweet and charming he was.

Oh, how they both tugged at her heart.

This is not the way she had expected things to turn out. She could never have fathomed sitting here, at the dressing table, smiling with loving fondness as her husband did everything in his power to soothe their baby.

No, not their baby. His baby.

It was the same as having a bucket of cold water dumped over her head.

She had no place here, not really. No marriage license, no ring, would make her truly part of this world.

And that was as it should be, was it not?

"Promise me something," she whispered.

"Anything." He glanced her way, one eyebrow quirked.

Promise me you'll be good to her. Promise you won't forget me when this is over. That once it comes time to build my theater, you won't give the work to someone else to manage in your stead. Promise you'll let me visit from time to time.

How could she hope to share what he'd brought to life inside her? Something far deeper than anything she'd ever read or seen on stage. Something real, something that hurt and thrilled her all at once. Whenever he looked at her with his crooked little smile, as he did at that moment while lifting Violet into his arms—in spite of his fine evening suit of clothes and the damage the baby might do —Cate simply forgot to breathe.

No, there was no chance of sharing her conflicted feelings. Not if she wished to avoid making him uncomfortable, perhaps even making him resent her. She couldn't stand that.

"Do not make me perform tonight. Please, no recitations. My nerves simply couldn't take it." She rubbed her trembling hands together, her distress nearly too much to bear.

He left the baby then, going to her and sinking to one knee. "Cate, that was all in fun. I would never ask you to do anything that would cause you such distress. The last thing I wish to do is to distress you."

What he did not know was that the entire situation distressed her, from beginning to end, and that falling to one knee before her was both the best and worst thing he could have done, for now, she longed to fall into his arms.

There was so much more than that, as if her feelings for him weren't enough. She admired and respected his mother and disgusted herself by wearing the ring which had previously been worn in love. Knowing this was nothing more than a sham, really, disrespectful toward true marriage. Toward true love.

A creeping suspicion which made itself evident to her as he took her hands gazed deep into her eyes. The suspicion as she stared into their blue depths that she wished this was real.

How terribly unfortunate for her soon-to-be-disappointed heart.

He knew none of this as he tried to bolster her. "You have done tremendously up to this point, and I have nothing but faith that you will continue to perform admirably. Just think of all the practice you've had now, all of the experience to apply toward the many roles you will play once your theater is complete."

She knew this was supposed to comfort her, that it was intended to remind her of why she'd embarked upon this in the first place. Yet it did little to soothe the ache in her chest, nor did it make smaller the lump in her throat.

There was nothing to be done but to remind herself that this was, in fact, a part she was playing. Not only was she performing for his parents, but she was performing for him, as well. She put on a brilliant smile as she stood, going to the crib to remove Violet from it once again. "Your grandmother will wish to see you," she murmured to the baby, who smiled so charmingly and embedded herself more firmly in Cate's affections.

"You look lovely tonight," Landon observed with an approving smile.

"Thank you. I thought it would be nice to impress your parents a bit." She held her free arm out to the side, turning slowly in place that he might admire her in detail. Blue watered silk, nearly the same shade as his eyes, cut fashionably low in the front and high in the back, the collar standing straight up.

"You are the very image of beauty," he murmured, and there was a depth in his voice which had not been there before. An intimacy. She could feel her blood racing, could hear the thumping in her chest grow stronger when he drew nearer.

"Thank you," she managed to choke out.

"Standing there, holding the baby..." He let out a long sigh, his brow furrowing. "I wish..."

What he wished, she never found out.

For a cry from the first floor sent them both running from the room.

"Mother?" Landon shouted on his way down, and Cate followed him to the parlor where his mother appeared to be having a fit.

"What is this?" Cate asked, aghast, wondering for a moment if this was the nature of Hermione's illness. She wept violently, hands over her face, shaking from head to toe.

Landon did not appear to understand any better than she did. He turned to his father, who stood off to the side, and to his credit, he appeared stricken at the sight of his wife's distress. "What happened? Why is she upset?"

Oliver handed him a telegram. "This just came. An

emergency in Washington. They need me back there immediately."

Cate didn't know whether to cheer or weep right alongside Hermione. "Oh, my goodness," she whispered, holding Violet close while Landon attempted to comfort his mother.

This was it, then. The end. So soon.

And she should have been glad. She should have rejoiced. There was no longer anything to worry about— she could even go home and no longer fear for her sisters or the ranch.

And she would have her theater, for good and for all. Finally.

Why, then, did her tears fall on Violet's lace-trimmed gown? Why did she want to hold the baby tighter than ever?

Rather than do this, she went to Hermione. "Why don't you hold her?" she asked, sitting beside her. "Spend time with her while you can. I will help get your things together if that makes things easier."

Hermione lowered her hands, her face tear-stained and swollen. "Oh, my dear," she whimpered. "How did you know just the right thing to say?"

She bit her lip to hold back a broken cry. "Because that is what I would want more than anything," she admitted, placing a hand on the woman's back in what she hoped was a comforting manner.

"We can't possibly leave until first thing in the morning," Oliver announced, and it was clear to Cate that he was trying to make this as easy on his wife as possible.

It was all for naught, as she was far too upset. "I do not understand why we have to go. Just yesterday evening you suggested staying through Christmas, and now you tell me we have to go tomorrow morning. I'm so tired of always having this emergency or that emergency to tend to."

Oliver appeared stunned by this admission, as did Landon.

Cate, however, was not surprised. She knew she would feel similarly where she in her mother-in-law's place. While she did not know their situation well, she understood it clearly enough feel her frustration, her fatigue.

It seemed Mr. Jenkins was unable to conduct his political life without his wife by his side. Or perhaps he simply did not wish to be away from her. But it was a terrible lot to ask of a woman who was reportedly in poor health.

Cate had to wonder if that poor health had anything to do with always being on a train, or in a hotel. Perhaps she simply needed time to rest.

It saddened her to think she could not offer her mother-in-law a place in her home. She may have stayed there with them, watching over the baby and relaxing, enjoying the fresh air she seemed to love so well.

Yet that could not be, for in the end, it was better for everyone involved if the Jenkins left on the first train east.

She sensed Landon's conflicted feelings about the matter, as well. He appeared pained. His face screwed up in a grimace. She knew him well enough by now to know how it pained him to see her this way, knowing he ought to help her but being unable to do so.

"There, there. There will be more chances for you to visit, and for Violet to visit you. You will always be her grandmother." Cate kissed her tear-stained cheek and wished she could say something, anything to ease the woman's pain. Her disappointment.

"We had better go upstairs to get my things packed." The resignation in Hermione's voice spoke volumes. She carried Violet up the stairs, with Cate following behind.

It appeared as though her troubles were over now.

Why in the world was she so unhappy?

21

It was so difficult to be happy and relieved when his mother was so desperately disappointed.

Oliver threw his hands into the air, turning toward the fire. "What am I supposed to do? She ought to understand by now that I cannot control when I am needed. Does she not believe I would rather live in a home like this? That I would rather have a set schedule, times of day in which I knew I would be with my family? I would love nothing more than to have what you have here."

He bowed his head, removing his spectacles to wipe them on his handkerchief, and Landon wished he knew what to say. His father had never been so frank with him. He'd always imagined the man enjoyed his travels, his meetings and speeches, and conferences. Never had it occurred to him that the great Oliver Jenkins would much rather live at home and enjoy a quiet life.

The thought that he envied his son for something which was not real only deepened Landon's sympathy.

"Perhaps you had better speak to her."

Oliver snickered. "It is clear you have not been married for long."

"What is that supposed to mean?"

"It is for the best that she get this out of her system. Speaking with your wife will help her calm herself, as will being with the baby. Once she has had some time to herself, I will go to her. At the moment, she wants nothing to do with me, and anything I say will only make things worse. Have you not found that to be the case?"

He poured a drink for both of them, thinking this over. "Yes, I suppose there's something to be said for that. It is better for both parties to step away and get their thoughts in order before possibly making things worse."

"Precisely." Oliver accepted his whiskey with a thoughtful expression. "Son, do you think she resents me?"

This was not at all the sort of conversation they'd ever had before. Landon never would have guessed his father thought along these lines. "I don't think so. She has always stood beside you. Perhaps she is tired, or it was only this disappointment speaking when she became upset."

"Everyone has their limits, son." He stared down into his drink, swirling it in the glass. "I'm afraid she might have reached hers. I wish there was something I could do. We shall have to return for another visit just as soon as possible."

Landon suddenly felt as though his collar was too tight.

He could not imagine going through this all over again, and if his parents returned to find him divorced, things would only get worse.

What else was there to say? "Yes, whenever you can."

How foolish he'd been, imagining this would ever come to an end. Now that he had a child, his mother would never accept his divorce without quite a bit of pestering and questioning and, undoubtedly, more than a few tears. He supposed he could announce their separation via letter, and thus be spared the brunt of her emotions.

He would hate himself while writing.

"If you wish, I could go to the train station for you, perhaps secure your tickets for the morning."

Oliver shook his head, downing his drink before returning the glass. "I shall do it. I need fresh air. Perhaps by the time I return, your mother will be sufficiently recovered so as to talk this over as adults."

Landon might not have been married for long, but even he knew the folly of using such language. He hoped his father would not make his mother out to be a child when he returned, for that would only upset her more than ever. No adult wished to be treated as a child for simply feeling as any person would.

This brought Cate to mind, and how often she'd been treated as a child. How eager she'd been to prove herself as something more. And how well she'd managed to do just that.

Before he ascended the stairs to check on the women, Mrs. Davis left the kitchen and walked down the hall.

"Is there anything I can do?" she whispered, wide-eyed and embarrassed for him.

He shook his head with as much of a smile as he could muster. "I suppose you might keep supper warm in the kitchen, though I doubt either of my parents are in the mood to eat now."

The fact was, he hardly had an appetite himself. Not only was he too concerned for his mother, but he suddenly found himself at the end of his short-lived marriage. What a sudden turn of events.

He understood then, as he climbed the stairs, that he had truly been looking forward to another week or two of this. Knowing her room was just beside his, where he might speak privately with her. Sharing meals with her, looking forward to her charming sense of humor and bright conversation.

The simple pleasure of kissing her cheek before entering the bank that morning had opened his eyes to a life he'd believed himself far above. Beyond the clutches of marriage and domestic life.

If he'd given it any thought before, he would have imagined spending the rest of his life as a bachelor, dining with friends and occasionally sporting a young woman about town.

Now? How could he ever go back to that way of living? Even with a governess, someone to watch over Violet while he did as he pleased, it would never be the same. His heart would no longer be in it.

Not when his heart was at home, with his daughter.

Wishing he had someone like Cate to greet him at the end of the day.

No, not someone like her. Cate herself. No one else would do now.

As if she heard him thinking about her, she emerged from the back bedroom when he reached the landing. The strain on her lovely face tugged at his heart. "How is she? And, how are you?"

The poor girl appeared to have aged in only a few minutes, lines evident on her forehead and beside her eyes. Her mouth drooped at the corners. "She is still very upset, and I have managed to pack most of her things."

"But, how are you?" He took her by the hand, leading her further down the hall toward their rooms. They could speak more freely there, without fear of being overheard. "I would imagine this has brought you some measure of relief."

For some reason, unfair as it was, he almost wanted her to tell him no, this did not bring her relief. That she felt as he did. That he had brought something to her life just as she brought something to his.

But how could that be true? He was merely a means to an end for her. The money she needed to make her dreams a reality.

Her thoughts did not lie along the lines his did. Then again, he had never been aware of the sweetness missing in his life until she had become part of it. Was there a chance...?

Cate nodded, the creases in her forehead deepening

when she frowned. "It has, I suppose. Though I will miss her."

It was now or never. He could be brave, or he could be a coward. "Just her?" he whispered, hoping against hope.

Her eyes met his, then darted away. "I wish you wouldn't do this."

"Wish I wouldn't what?" Something had changed, something had come between them in the time since he'd admired her in her room, when he'd been on the verge of kissing her, or at least telling her how much he longed to do so.

He'd been so certain of her affections then, or at least of the fact that she wanted him to kiss her. He'd seen that wide-eyed look before, had heard the breathless little gasp when a woman found it difficult to breathe in front of a man she admired.

Now, she appeared prepared to cut him down to size. "Is this what you do? Do you toy with the affections of young women? When you know you have no intention of following through?"

His mind reeled. This was the last thing he'd expected. Even her expression hardened as she looked up at him. "I don't understand. All this time..."

She shook her head, her eyes harder than he had ever seen them. "You have what you want now. Your parents are of the belief that you have family. You can go on with your life. You can help me with mine. What else is there? You do not need to complicate this. Frankly, I would rather not be left by the wayside when your work takes you elsewhere."

As always, he felt as though she were two steps ahead of him. All he could do was scramble to keep up. "It would not be that way. Not the way it is with my parents."

"Yes, but you were away for a year. You are an important man, I would imagine—" She looked away, folding her arms. "This is all for naught. I don't know why I let my imagination get away from me. Isn't that what you've already accused me of?"

"Why are you so angry? What have I done?" When she would not face him, he took her by the shoulders and turned her in place. "Look at me when I speak to you. At least do me that favor."

He was surprised to find tears standing in her eyes. Little wonder she had wished to avoid his gaze. His irritation melted in the face of her emotion, softening him, making him eager to soothe her. "Cate, I'm afraid I don't understand what's truly happening here. I don't know what I've done to make you so angry, when that is the last thing I ever wish to do. Please, talk to me."

His hands tightened around her shoulders, and he drew her a bit closer. How he longed to hold her, to comfort her and promise that whatever she believed about him was not true.

The door to the back bedroom opened, and his mother emerged. He released Cate quickly, as if her shoulders burned beneath his hands.

"I know this might sound terribly strange, but would you mind moving the baby's crib into my room tonight? I would like very much to have the chance to care for her one last time before we go."

Cate's anger dissolved in an instant, her expression softening as she smiled at his mother. "Of course. Anything you wish."

Hermione chuckled. "I would imagine it would make things easier for you tonight, as well. You might enjoy a good night's sleep."

A good night's sleep?

How would he ever manage that now that Cate hated him for some reason he could not begin to understand?

22

She knew she was merely going through the motions as she groomed herself the following morning, washing her face clean of the dried tears which had accumulated over a long, sleepless night.

She brushed her hair after freeing it from its braid, then coiled it into a heavy bun on the back of her head and pinned it in place.

This was the last time she need pretend to be the happy wife and mother. She knew it ought to come as a great relief, just as she had known since the night before.

Perhaps she would be relieved if she did not feel as though she were on the verge of losing something she had never truly possessed.

How many times had she gazed at the ring on her left hand in the glow from the fire, wishing it were truly the symbol it was meant to be?

How many times had she cursed herself for being so cross with Landon?

She'd been afraid, nothing more. For she did not wish to ever be that woman, the one weeping as her husband told her where to go and when to be there.

Just a few minutes spent with Hermione, listening to her resigned sighs and sniffling, had reminded her of the perils of ever being beholden to a man for any reason.

Yet Landon had done nothing to deserve her ire or her fear. She'd spent the night wishing for the courage to knock on his door and offer apologies. Pride would not allow it, nor would modesty.

But it had been mostly pride, plain and simple.

She heard Violet babbling and cooing in the hall before Hermione knocked, and she resolved to be cheerful when she opened the door to them.

"Good morning," she fairly sang, "and how was she last night?"

"I believe you are correct, but then, you would be. Mothers normally are." Hermione handed Violet over with a regretful little sigh. "The women you hired to care for Violet must not have properly helped her after feeding. How could any baby sleep soundly while suffering from an uncomfortable air bubble in their stomach?"

"That is exactly what I had suspected." Cate nuzzled Violet's soft cheek, glad she'd at least understood what was wrong with the baby even if she was not her baby.

But oh, how she wished it were so. That it had been motherly intuition rather than simple common sense.

"How are you?" she asked, noting the dark circles beneath her mother-in-law's eyes.

Hermione's smile was rather grim, but triumphant. "I believe my husband and I now understand each other. He knows I'm terribly disappointed and has promised we might return at the earliest convenience."

Cate's heart clenched, though she gave as little indication of it as she could manage. What would Landon do in that case? She decided that was for him to worry about, for she had other concerns to manage. His life was not her life, and she would do well to remember that.

"I'm sure nothing would give us more pleasure," she lied. It was not a lie told with malice or out of any desire to mislead, but rather as a means of sparing the woman's feelings. She was already suffering enough, and did not need to know there would be no daughter-in-law waiting for her when she returned.

They descended the stairs together, and Cate reflected on how this would be the last morning she would spend here. What would Violet do when she was gone? For a moment, she considered asking Landon if he would allow her to bring the baby to the ranch until he found someone to care for her on a steady basis, but that would only deepen their connection and would, therefore, make it all the more difficult to let go of her when the time came.

Once again, she reminded herself that this was not her life. She could not over-concern herself with the lives of those who would shut her out when the time came.

Breakfast had been laid out in the morning room by the

efficient Mrs. Davis, and Cate poured coffee for Hermione and herself.

"I understand your train leaves at 10 o'clock," she murmured as she went about the business of serving the food.

"Yes. My husband shall be down to dine with us in a moment. I understand Landon went to the bank to inform Mr. Witherspoon that he would be taking the morning off to spend with us."

"Yes, he did." In reality, Cate had not the slightest idea what he'd done, as they had not spoken since their unfortunate encounter in the hall.

She did wish for the chance to apologize, though she was afraid she had destroyed any chance of even friendship between them. Perhaps that was for the best. She was not certain she could never be friends with him when she wanted to be so much more. They were business partners, nothing more than that.

Oliver entered the room, immediately going to Violet. "I hope the next time we visit, the two of us have a chance to get to know each other better," he said as he lifted her from Cate's arms.

She hoped the same, for both their sakes. They deserved to get to know each other better.

She turned away, looking out the window. It was all too much. Tears threatened to flow at any time.

It was never truly yours. They are not yours. Violet isn't yours, and neither is Landon.

There was a knock at the front door, causing them all to look at each other.

"Perhaps Landon forgot his key," Hermione suggested, rising as if to answer.

"Don't worry yourself. I will attend to it." It was an excuse to get out of the room, anyway. Cate hurried down the hall, waving Mrs. Davis away as she made a move as if to answer instead.

It was not Landon outside, nor was it anyone Cate recognized. "Yes?" she asked, waiting.

The young woman blinked rapidly, staring with an open mouth. "Who are you?" she demanded upon regaining control of herself.

This was unexpected. Strangers did not typically arrive on a doorstep and make demands. Cate stammered, "I— that is, I might ask you the same question. I am Mrs. Jenkins. This is my home. Once again, I ask, who are you?"

"Where is Landon?"

A sinking suspicion planted its roots in Cate's belly. It was the girl's fair hair which made her wonder... "I assume you mean Mr. Jenkins. Might I say who is calling?"

The girl raised her chin in defiance, looking every inch the queen in spite of her rather ragged appearance. Her coat was worn at the elbows and a bit too tight at the waist.

More than likely she had been unable to afford a new coat after gaining weight. A corset could only do so much after a woman had given birth.

"You might tell him Ida Thomas is calling." Her raised

voice must have inspired Hermione and Oliver to inspect their visitor, and Ida stared at them over Cate's shoulder. "And if he knows what's good for him, he will let me see my baby."

Cate held onto the door to keep herself from swooning and sliding to the floor.

"What is the meaning of this?" Oliver demanded, marching up to them. "What you mean, your baby?"

"Just as I say. That baby is mine."

"Oliver, please. Do not upset the girl. Perhaps you had better go alert the authorities, for she is surely disturbed."

Cate glanced over her shoulder to find Hermione backing further down the hall, holding Violet close.

"What is this all about?" Oliver turned to Cate. "Do you know this girl?"

She managed to find her voice. "No, I cannot say that I do."

"I don't know her, either, but I can assure you, she is not Mrs. Jenkins. She is not that baby's mother. Violet is my baby."

Oliver sputtered. "You know her name?"

Ida scoffed. "I ought to know. I named her."

There were footsteps on the stairs behind her, and soon Landon came into view. His face fell when he saw what took place before him. For the briefest moment, Cate wondered if he would turn tail and run.

"Son, what is this about?" Oliver stepped out onto the porch, hands on his hips. "Someone had better explain this, and quickly."

They had come so close. So close to ending this without anyone being terribly hurt.

Cate looked at Ida, beckoning with one curled hand. "Come inside. I believe the two of us ought to have a talk."

Ida smirked, looking her up and down. "Why would I want to talk with you? You've been pretending Violet is yours, and pretending you are married to this man."

"I am married to this man," Cate retorted. "Still, I believe there are things we ought to speak about. Please, come inside." The fact was, she had no idea what she would say to the girl. She only knew how important it was to get her off the porch and out of public view. It would not do for a scandal to start up over this.

She went to the parlor, closing the doors behind her once Ida joined her. Out in the hall, Oliver peppered Landon with questions while Hermione exclaimed in surprise.

That was Landon's problem. She wanted to die of shame, and nothing she said or did at this point would make any difference.

"What is it you want to talk about, then?" Ida asked, looking about the room. "He's changed things."

Cate let this pass, willing herself not to imagine this girl sitting in this room with him. "What brings you back? How could you abandon your daughter that way? Do you know he wanted to make things right with you, but could not because you ran away? It might have been you here in this house instead of me. He might have been able to have his true family, not some false front."

"So you admit you aren't his wife?"

"Oh, no, I am his wife. We were married. But that is beside the point now. What brings you back? And why did you leave?"

"I'll tell you why she came back."

Cate jumped in shock. Somehow, in the midst of all the chaos, Mason had found his way into the house and now stood there, watching her. He had even managed to open the parlor door without her noticing.

"Mason! How did you know... I mean, what brings you..."

"Let's just say someone asked me to look into Miss Thomas and her movements." He turned away from Cate and focused on Ida, a faint smile playing at the corners of his mouth. "It seems you fled Carson City while in the company of a young man. The young man abandoned you in Kansas City, which led you to return here. You needed money, badly, and chose to return to Mr. Jenkins's home in hopes of blackmailing him into paying your way elsewhere. If he refused, you planned to tell the entire town that his child had been born out of wedlock and that he had lied to his parents to avoid a scandal. Is that not the long and short of it?"

His thoroughness took Cate's breath away, and clearly had a similar effect on Ida.

The girl's already pale skin turned shades whiter, her cheeks draining of color. "H—how do you know?"

"You had best learn not to share secrets with girls in a boardinghouse. Especially girls in situations similar to yours, who are so in need of money that they are willing to share your secrets with anyone who can provide them with a dollar or two."

He opened his topcoat just enough to reveal his deputy's badge. "You do know blackmail as a crime, do you not? And that the information I collected on you provides grounds with which I might place you under arrest? I'm sure the judge will not look kindly on your scheme."

Cate found herself feeling sorry for the girl as her eyes welled with tears which soon spilled over.

"I only—that is, I needed—I could not manage her on my own, and he told me he would take care of me…"

Cate went to her, draping an arm around her shoulders. "I'm sorry for what you've been through," she murmured, meaning it with all her heart.

Ida looked at her in shock, her mouth falling open. "How can you say that to me? After what I came here intending to do?"

"I have always been able to sense the motivations of others. I feel the pain of your situation quite keenly, and I cannot imagine doing anything differently were I in your place."

She turned to Mason, silently pleading with him. He lifted his brows, and she lifted a shoulder in a shrug. There seemed no reason to arrest the girl, when not true harm had been done.

Well, no harm aside from the grief this revelation must have caused Mr. and Mrs. Jenkins.

"Perhaps you had best discuss this with Landon," she suggested.

"Perhaps I had better," Mason agreed. "In the meantime, since he seems a bit... preoccupied, I suggest Miss Thomas come with me to the jailhouse. You will not be under arrest, strictly, but I would like to hold you in place until Mr. Jenkins decides whether to take this to the judge."

He took Ida's arm, turning to Cate before leading her from the house. "I don't think I need to tell you that you have quite a bit of explaining to do," he murmured, one eyebrow quirking up.

"No. You don't need to tell me." She watched as Mason and Ida left together, with Ida weeping into a handkerchief all the while.

Meanwhile, Landon's voice raised in protest in the morning room, and Cate made it a point to dash up the stairs before any of them could notice her.

It would be better to leave as quickly as possible, for the sooner she put this behind her, the sooner she could move on with her life and forget the humiliation she had suffered this day.

23

"How could you do such a thing?" Oliver walked the length of the room, his hands clasped behind his back while Hermione wept softly, her cheek against the top of Violet's head.

Landon had never known such humiliation was possible. Not as an adult, at least. Here he was, a grown man, suffering one insult after another.

The worst of it was, he felt most keenly for Cate. What his parents must've thought of her. He could manage their disdain, their disappointment. But she did not deserve any of it.

"As I told you, I wished to make things right with the girl, but she ran away. The only thing I could imagine doing was to pretend Cate was the child's natural mother."

"And she went along with this?" Oliver roared.

"Hush," Hermione chided him. When his eyes flew open wide—as did Landon's, for it was rare to hear her offer an opinion on anything he did, at least in public—she continued, "You are upsetting the baby, and you are upsetting me. Regardless of whether or not she was born in wedlock, she is still our grandchild. And perhaps if you were a bit more understanding, our son would never have felt the need to mislead us this way."

This was an entirely new side Hermione which neither man had seen before.

"I hope you are not trying to say you approve of what our son has done?" Oliver gasped. "Why, this goes against everything we taught him."

He whirled on Landon, teeth bared in a snarl. "Did I not always advise you to behave like a gentleman?"

"Could we not discuss this so frankly front of my mother?"

"Your mother is a grown woman, and you are a grown man, as am I. We are all adults here, and since you have exposed us to this terrible scandal, it seems only fitting that we discuss it."

"There is nothing to discuss. I knew you would react this way, and I wished to ease things for everyone involved."

His mother spoke up again. "Is Cate truly your wife?"

Landon nodded. "Yes, I did marry her. I wanted that to be true, if nothing else. Our understanding was that we would end the marriage and I would provide her with the money she needs to start a business of her own."

Oliver's eyes widened as if he'd found the key to everything. "Aha! This was all about money. I should have known. The mercenary little thing, pretending to be a fine young woman while all along she had one hand in your billfold."

If it were not his father speaking to him this way, Landon might have entertained the notion of strangling him with his bare hands. As it was, they curled into fists at his sides as he stared down his father. "I'll have you know, it was my idea all along. I pulled her into this with the promise of financial reward, knowing how much she longed to build a theater in Carson City. I saw an opportunity, and I seized it. Isn't that what you always taught me, Father?"

Oliver's cheeks reddened. "So this is my fault, then?"

"Not at all. I simply thought you would understand if I put the matter in terms with which you were more familiar. Cate is blameless in all of this. She only wished to make everyone happy, and I believe she truly cares for Violet."

Hermione nodded, wiping away a tear. "Yes, I sense that as well. I sense a great many things. I must admit, though you may not believe it, it seemed to be from the start there was something strange between the two of you. And that she did not seem quite as comfortable here as she should have been. But I do not doubt the purity of her heart."

He went to her, using his handkerchief to wipe away the rest of her tears with a tender, grateful smile. "I do not doubt it, either. She has suffered a great deal today, and I hope to make it up to her."

"Go to her, then." Hermione took his hand, squeezing. "She's a lovely girl. If you care for her, do not let her get away."

"I cannot fathom this!" his father exploded.

"No, Oliver." His mother sighed. "I suspect you cannot."

Without a look at his father, Landon burst from the room. "Cate?" he called out, looking from one room to the other. Both she and Ida had disappeared.

He bounded up the stairs two at a time, still calling for her and still receiving no answer. When he went to her room, he found her things still waiting, but she was not there with them.

He had almost left the room and was about to return to the first floor when he noticed the folded piece of paper on the dressing table. When he picked it up and unfolded it, something fell out onto the floor.

He looked down, his chest tightening when he recognized the ring he'd given her.

I will send for my belongings shortly. Please, tell your parents goodbye for me, and tell your mother I hope she will forgive me for wearing this ring when I had no right to do so.

That was it. Nothing personal for him, not the slightest hint of anything else she might have felt. He supposed that meant she had never felt anything else at all.

His mother reached the top of stairs, finding him standing in the doorway with the ring in one hand and the note in the other. It must've been evident from his expression that he'd lost her.

Her face fell. "What are you going to do?"

"What is there to do? She's gone. I wouldn't know where to begin." He closed his fist around the ring, aching and sorrowful and very much of the feeling that he'd just been run over by a speeding train. There had still been time to repair things between them, or at least that was what he'd told himself when he could not sleep the night before. That he would find a way to make things right.

There had been no accounting for Ida's sudden presence, or the way she would humiliate Cate and himself. It was not that he cared for his own humiliation, but hers? He would have moved heaven and earth if it meant avoiding causing her even a moment's discomfort.

His mother sighed, coming to him and taking his face in her hands. "It does seem as though you've gotten yourself into a terrible mess," she murmured, mournful.

He could only laugh at himself, but there was no humor in his laughter. "Yes, it would appear as though I have."

It seemed no matter how old he got, no matter how many years he spent managing his own affairs and conducting his own business, there was something about the probing, knowing gaze of his mother which left him open to her scrutiny and understanding. "I did not raise you to stand back and admit defeat without at least making an effort to avail yourself."

"You did, however, teach me how to accept defeat gracefully. I will not make a fool of myself, not even for her."

Now she was every inch his mother, fixing him with a stern expression. "Why not? She made a fool of herself for you."

Her words chilled him to the bone. He wished she wasn't right though he knew she was. Cate had risked quite a lot for him. Her reputation, her standing among her sisters, even the ranch—if word of her marriage were to get out and be used against her.

And here he was, cowering like a child, hiding in his home for fear of facing her once more. Leave it to his mother to put it all so plainly.

"Even if I were to find her, what would I say? How could I convince her how much I care?"

She beamed. "You do care, though?"

"Oh, Mother. You have no idea."

"I suspect I do. Don't be fooled by your old, tired parents. I suspect such depth of emotion is limited to the young, but the memory does not fade. I remember all too well feeling as if my heart would burst from my chest whenever your father entered the room. Even after we were married, I would sometimes forget to breathe when he came too close."

Landon could scarcely imagine such a time ever taking place, though it was a comfort to know his mother understood. "I did wish to spare you all of this," he murmured. "I'm so sorry."

A brief frown crossed her face, creasing her brow. "I cannot pretend to approve of the situation as a whole, but these things do happen. I now have a beautiful granddaughter who is truly the light of my life. I cannot be entirely disapproving."

He gathered her up in a tight hug, joyful in spite of the hole in his chest which Cate had left.

"Now," she said after freeing herself and brushing off his shoulders and chest, "I ask again. What are you going to do about this? Are you going to allow her to leave, never sharing your true feelings?"

"It isn't as if I will never see her again. We are business partners now, and I fully intend to see this through. I will not renege on our agreement."

"No, it will be too late by then. What you intend to do? Confess what lies in your heart, days or even weeks from now? By then it might be too late. She might have turned away from you completely. At the very least, it will be terribly awkward to revisit the situation."

He saw the sense in this, and knew it left him with only one clear option.

Yet another knock at the door, and Landon groaned. "I feel as though I live in a train station," he grumbled as they made their way down the stairs.

Mrs. Davis was already on her way to receive their caller.

Landon immediately recognized Sheriff Connelly on the porch.

"Come in," Landon invited. "Mother, this is Sheriff Connelly."

Rance removed his hat, tipping his head in her direction. "Ma'am, I'm pleased to meet you. I thought you should know that Miss Thomas is at the jailhouse, and we are waiting to find whether you wish to go ahead with charging her with attempted blackmail. My deputy—"

Landon frowned. "Blackmail? I don't know anything about this."

"Cate didn't tell you before she left?"

His heart skipped a beat. "You saw her? You saw her before she left?"

"Yes, she asked me to secure a ride for her to the ranch. She came to the jailhouse not long after Mason brought Miss Thomas in. I assumed you knew the details of the situation." He offered a brief explanation, which left Hermione gasping in shock.

Landon did not gasp. The entire thing made perfect sense to him. "No, I do not wish to press charges against her. What's done is done."

His mother tugged his sleeve. "What if she decides to come back for the baby? She is her mother, after all."

"I would like to see her try." He turned to the sheriff. "And you say Cate went home?"

He nodded, looking decidedly more concerned now. "Yes, she did. She was in quite a state, if you do not mind my saying."

Landon explained, "Sheriff Connelly is Cate's brother-in-law, and I suspect he is none too pleased with me."

To his surprise, his mother merely waved this off. "Do not worry, Sheriff. My son is going to make everything right."

"And how does he plan to do that?"

Landon nodded. "Yes, mother. Please tell me. How do I intend to make things right?"

She laughed. "You will see. Now, get yourself dressed, and see to it that you look well. I shall dress the baby. We are going on a call."

"But your train!"

"That can wait. I will not leave my son until he has found a way to straighten this out." She marched to the morning room, where Landon could overhear her informing her husband that they would wait another day before leaving for Washington.

He knew not where this strength and determination had suddenly come from, but it seemed that being needed had invigorated her.

Landon turned to the sheriff with a shrug. "You see how much say I have in this."

Sheriff Connelly replaced his hat, grimacing slightly as he did. "If you intend to make a call at the ranch, allow me to warn you that you might have to work your way through a few screeching sisters in order to reach your wife."

Landon recalled his surprise meeting with Molly, chuckling as he did. "I would expect nothing less."

24

———

Cate walked up the porch steps in a daze. Her legs carried her of their own accord, without her telling them to do so.

All she wanted in the world was to lock herself in her bedchamber and never, ever emerge again.

If only she could sleep and be alone. If only everyone would leave her alone.

She knew better than to expect any such thing, for the moment she stepped through the door she was descended upon at once.

They fired questions at her, their voices overlapping as they removed her coat and hat.

"Where have you been?"

"What brings you back?"

"What happened?"

"You look a fright!"

"Are you ill?"

"Did something happen to you?"

She stood in the center of this, swaying slightly. Looking at them but not truly seeing them. All she could see was Landon and Violet. Just the thought of them was like a hand closing around her throat, squeezing until she could not breathe.

They would never understand this. They all had what they wanted, who they wanted. Who they loved.

How had she ever believed herself to be above the sort of love they knew? She'd always thought of herself first as an actress, unable to tie herself down with such petty concerns. She'd certainly not intended to lose her heart as she had.

Strangely, Molly seemed to understand best. With an arm around Cate's waist, she led her to the stairs. "It seems you need a great deal of rest," she murmured, gentle and soft.

"Do you not even wish to know where I have been?"

Molly scoffed. "Do you honestly not think I knew where you are? Why do you think I had Mason look for that Ida Thomas?"

Cate stopped halfway up the stairs, her mouth falling up in surprise. Not many things could have shaken her from her stupor. "That was you? How did you know?"

"So he made good on his promise," Molly murmured, smiling to herself. "Let us say I have met your husband."

"Please don't call him that."

Molly shrugged, offering no reply, and they continued up the stairs. Somehow, she had spoken with him. She understood. At the very least, she tried to understand and to be gentle with Cate. That was more than enough to be grateful for.

"I am so tired."

Molly opened her bedroom door and stepped aside to allow her in. Cate could have wept with relief at the sight of her own bed, her own washstand, her own dressing table. She supposed someone would have to go back for her clothing and such, but that could be arranged. Nothing had mattered so much as escaping before any blame-filled eyes had turned her way.

It would have been difficult enough saying goodbye to Landon and Violet without bearing up under the shame.

"How did it end?" Molly asked.

"As bad as it possibly could have. I do wish Mason had caught up to Ida before she arrived at the house and announced to all present that Violet was her baby." Cate sank onto the bed, bending to remove her shoes.

"She did not!" Molly gasped, I hand over her heart. "Of all the brazen, callous—"

"It doesn't matter now. I can only hope Landon settled things with his family."

"But you do not know whether or not he did?"

"I left before things were settled."

Molly fixed her with a stern look.

Cate shrugged. "What was I supposed to do?"

"You could not have run away, to begin with."

"That is easy for you to say. You do not know his parents. You did not come to care for his mother as I did. How was I supposed to bear her disappointment?"

"So, you left Landon to bear it alone."

"It was his to bear! I am not the one who brought the child into the world. It was not I who came up with the notion of lying to spare them the embarrassment of an illegitimate grandchild. What was I to do?"

"He cares for you, you know."

Cate scoffed, shaking her head. "No, he doesn't. Now that everything is over, he doesn't need me anymore."

"I would not discount him so quickly if I were you. He impressed me a great deal when I went to see him. He gave me quite an earful about you, too."

Though Cate did her best to close her heart off to this, to build a wall around herself that nothing could penetrate, curiosity soon got the best of her. "What did he say?" she asked, averting her gaze that her sister might not know how eager she was.

"He told me I never gave enough you credit, that none of us did. That he trusted you with his daughter, that he trusted you completely. He told me what a fine person you are, and how well you handled yourself up to that point. He admires you a great deal."

While this warmed her considerably, it did not mean anything real. "Admiring someone is not the same as truly caring for them."

Molly shrugged. "That could be so, but I have my suspicions." She crossed the room, sitting beside Cate on the bed and taking her hand. "What he said made me think. I have not been fair to you. None of us have. We all should have known better than to attempt to dissuade you from your intended course of action. You have always been the most determined person I've ever known, and I respect that," she added. "That is not meant to disparage you in any way. I admire your determination a great deal, along with your imagination and your talent and your open, loving heart. I have never said these things, not even when you were sick. Remember? When you ran away when we first got here?"

Cate chuckled ruefully. "How could I forget? I lost my sight for a short time."

"I was so afraid I lost you then, but it took no time for me to fall straight back into my old habits. Being hard on you, so stern and disinclined to understand your desires. Forgive me for that, please."

Cate hugged her impulsively. "There's nothing to forgive. I can only imagine how difficult I've made things for you, for all of you."

"Now we have you back, which is a blessing at least. The house is not been the same without you."

Yes, she was back, and things could go on as they had before. She was far too distraught to even consider her theater at the moment. She supposed that could come about when she had gotten over her grief.

It just the thought of getting over him—of getting over both of them, Landon and the baby—was too much. She burst into tears, unable to conceal the depth of her disappointment any longer.

Instantly, her sisters joined them, surrounding her with love and understanding. Even in the depths of despair, she could appreciate the blessing of their love. Whether or not they agreed with her, they would always be there to bolster her when she needed them most.

"I don't know what to do without them!" she mourned. "I know, I know. I have made a great deal of excitement over very little in the past, but this is different. This is real."

Phoebe wiped away her tears, tears of her own standing in her eyes. "Perhaps all is not lost. Remember, I teased you at first. I suggested the possibility of a man such as Landon falling in love with you after your marriage. Perhaps he did!"

Cate sniffled, shaking her head. "Yes, I felt there might be a moment, but I think that was a matter of me convincing myself of what I wished were true. Surely he is glad to be rid of me now."

"You sound as if you are guessing," Holly informed her. "Did you ask him if he was glad to be rid of you?"

She shook her head again. "Of course not. I ran soon as I could. It was humiliating, his parents knowing what I had done."

Rachel clicked her tongue, shaking her head in disapproval. "That doesn't mean anything. What you did, you did for their son. If they had the nerve to condemn you for that, they are terrible people who do not deserve your patience or understanding."

"Too right," Molly agreed.

"I do wish I'd had the chance to say goodbye to the baby," she whispered. "I should have thought before I fled. I should have waited so I could say goodbye to her."

All five of them looked to the open door at the sound of commotion downstairs.

"What on earth?" Holly asked, rising from her kneeling position on the floor. "Is there any end to the excitement around here?"

"Cate!" It was Lewis, calling to her from downstairs. "You have a visitor!"

Her heart leapt, though she did what she could to keep it in place. No sense in getting herself excited. In fact, for all she knew Landon had thrown her things into a trunk and sent it behind her.

Even so, there was a great deal of murmuring and excitement as the girls descended the stairs and walked out to the porch.

She could not believe her eyes. A shining, black coach sat before the house, drawn by a pair of magnificent, snow-white horses. They pranced proudly, tossing their manes and swishing their tails, while someone opened the door from inside.

She let out a muffled sob as Landon stepped down from inside the coach, then turned and extended his arms. She saw Hermione lean out, handing Violet over to him.

Phoebe squeezed her arm. "I told you," she whispered excitedly.

Cate took one step forward on trembling legs, then another. "What are you doing here?" she asked.

"You might not know this about me, but I do not take well to people who run away before I have the chance to say what's on my mind."

She nodded, breathing deeply in a vain attempt to keep her pulse under control. It was like fighting a losing battle. "All right. What is on your mind? Now that you are here, what is it you wish to say?"

He looked behind her, his gaze traveling over her sisters. It was clear none of them had any intention of going inside, just as the coach containing his parents sat behind him. Whatever he had to say, he would say it in front of an audience.

He cleared his throat. "You left something behind at the house which belongs to you."

"I told you I would send for my things—"

He shook his head. "That is not what I meant. You left your ring." With his free hand, he reached into the pocket of his topcoat and withdrew the gold band. "I did not tell you I wished for it back. Why did you take it off?"

Did he not understand how this crushed her? How just the sight of him made it difficult to keep from collapsing into tears? Why did he insist on torturing her this way? "Because it isn't mine, not really."

"But it is. You are my wife, or have you forgotten?"

She looked over his shoulder to where his parents watched from inside the coach. Oliver at least had the decency to pretend he was not listening, though Hermione made no such effort. "I thought their train was at ten o'clock," she remembered.

"They decided to wait until tomorrow. They would not leave until this was settled." He thrust his hand toward her, still holding the ring. "I want you to have this. I want you to always have it."

"You could do better than that," Hermione hissed from inside the coach.

"I quite agree," Phoebe added from the porch.

He looked and sounded utterly harassed but continued. "I want you to wear this ring, and to be my wife. My real, true wife. I wanted to tell you that last night, but you made it impossible. I wanted to tell you that I did not want what we had to end simply because my parents were leaving."

She hardly dared believe it. "You did? You do?"

"Of course I do. I know ours has not been a conventional story, but I will never not be grateful that you came into my life. I thank providence for bringing you to me, but I know now that it is up to me to keep you by my side. And I want you by my side, always."

"What about my plans? About my dreams?"

She heard one of her sisters, perhaps more than one, gasp when she said this. She knew they would disapprove, but that was not her concern.

To his credit, he did not gasp or even appear surprised. "I want you to have what you want. If you want your theater, you shall have it. So long as I can, to have you. No, so long as we can, to have you." He looked down at Violet, who giggled as if she understood.

Cate was laughing and crying and rejoicing as she walked into his embrace, his arms around them both, while her sisters wept loudly and openly. Hermione sounded as though she was overwrought, as well, the sounds of happy tears coming from inside the coach.

Landon smiled down at her, and there was no longer any question as to the love in his gaze.

"I love you," he whispered. "I've loved you from the start, though I didn't know it for certain until I lost you. Please, don't ever leave me again."

"Never. Never, ever." She stood on tiptoe, close to his ear. "I love you, Landon Jenkins, and I am proud to be your wife."

He slid the gold band over her finger once again, before pulling her close. "And do not ever remove that again," he warned.

"I might."

"You what?" he gaped.

"Well, what if I'm called upon to play the part of an unmarried woman?"

His laughter was music. "Fair enough. I should have known."

He bent then, sweeping her up into their first true, proper kiss.

Not the brief kiss before the Justice of the Peace, nor a peck on the cheek for the sake of appearances.

This kiss left her clinging to him for fear she might fall, left her breathless and dizzy and wishing for nothing more than to kiss him every day for the rest of her life.

He was right.

Theirs had not been a conventional story.

They had married, and then had fallen in love.

Then again, what about her life ever been conventional?

"Now, all that's left is the matter of your signatures. All five Reed heiresses will sign here, on these lines." The lawyer dipped his pen into the inkwell. "Who would like to go first?"

All five of them looked to each other. "I suppose I should," Molly suggested. She handed baby Cordelia off to Lewis, who watched with great interest as his wife signed the deed to the ranch now that the will's terms had been fulfilled.

Next came Holly, holding Edward's hand. He was nearly three years old now and had attached himself to Holly. Rarely could she leave a room without him wanting to be with her. She signed her married name with a flourish, smiling up at her husband just after doing so.

Rachel followed next, her belly swollen with the babes she carried—Doc Perkins had heard two heartbeats when he'd last checked on her, and Mason had walked around like a man in a daze ever since. They'd just settled into their new home, one block away from Rance and Phoebe.

The only thing that could have gotten Phoebe out of the house at her advanced stage of pregnancy was the signing of the deed. She had only a handful of weeks to go and seemed to be counting the days. She signed her name, breathing a sigh of relief when she did. Yes, they were all relieved now that the thing was settled.

Cate was last. She looked to her sisters, all of them keenly aware of what this meant. They'd done what they had never imagined possible.

How could any of them have predicted the turn their lives would take? How, when they'd arrived in Carson City, could they know their husbands—their happiness—waited for them? At the time, it had been nothing but an inconvenience.

Now, it meant nothing less than their entire lives.

Cate looked down at the deed, seeing everything it symbolized. Their security, as Lewis had no intention of allowing anyone to buy what he still regarded as his land, the land he'd poured his life into. And none of them intended to sell, either, for they had all come to love it too dearly.

Little had their father known what he would set in motion when he'd willed his daughters across the country.

She signed her name. Catherine Reed Jenkins.

"That does it, then." She turned to Landon, who held Violet in the crook of his arm. The baby laughed, causing everyone in the lawyer's office to laugh along with her.

Even Mr. Brown chuckled as he reviewed the signatures and declared the matter settled.

They were landowners, the five of them, and need never fear again for the future of their ranch.

Cate knew Lewis hoped his children would one day take over, and Roan felt the same for Edward and any children he and Holly might be blessed with. It was in their blood, their love of the land, and that sort of love tended to carry on from one generation to the next.

"It seems there is a great celebration being prepared at the house," Lewis reminded them as they gathered themselves in preparation of setting out for the ranch. Their neighbors, the Beltons and Furnishes, had arranged a grand feast in honor of the signing of the deed. Ryan Belton's sister, Lena, had taken everything into her very capable hands, assuring them they need not worry about a thing.

Not a quarter mile from the lawyer's office sat the location of Cate's theater, where ground had just been broken a month earlier. The men were hard at work there, and she smiled with deep satisfaction when she imagined the palace that would soon rise where there was now nothing but empty space.

"You did it," Landon murmured, taking her arm as they walked to the carriage.

It was a beautiful day, much like the day they'd arrived on the train. To Cate, it seemed the entire world shone with a new freshness. New possibilities.

"We did it," she corrected him with a wink.

"And just think, in a year's time, you might be able to walk the stage in front of an audience."

She shrugged. "Perhaps. Perhaps not. It will be so soon after the baby is born."

He stopped short, pulling her to a stop alongside him. "Did you say…"

"The baby. Yes. Our baby." She stroked Violet's cheek. "You're going to have a brother or sister, darling."

He let out a roar of pure joy, causing others along the street to stare in surprise.

Cate didn't care.

Nothing mattered half as much as his elation. As their love.

The entire family climbed into their respective buggies and carriages and set off for the ranch and the celebration that was to come.

They had earned it, all of them.

Along with the many celebrations to come.

I hope you enjoyed
A Bargain for a Bride!

Click here for more Blythe Carver books!

Sign up for the newsletter to be notified of new releases.

Click on link for
Newsletter
or put this in your browser window:

landing.mailerlite.com/webforms/landing/p6l2s1

www.ingramcontent.com/pod-product-compliance
Lightning Source LLC
Chambersburg PA
CBHW020321160726
47992CB00004B/1634